NIGHT
of
POWER

ALSO BY ANAR ALI

Baby Khaki's Wings

ANAR ALI

NIGHT
of
POWER

VIKING

VIKING

an imprint of Penguin Canada, a division of Penguin Random House Canada Limited

Canada • USA • UK • Ireland • Australia • New Zealand • India • South Africa • China

First published 2019

*Publisher's note: This book is a work of fiction. Names, characters, places and incidents either
are the product of the author's imagination or are used fictitiously, and any resemblance
to actual persons living or dead, events, or locales is entirely coincidental.*

LIBRARY AND ARCHIVES CANADA CATALOGUING IN PUBLICATION

Title: Night of power / Anar Ali
Names: Ali, Anar, author.
Identifiers: Canadiana (print) 20190043547 | Canadiana (ebook) 20190043563 |
ISBN 9780670064267 (softcover) | ISBN 9780735234208 (PDF)
Classification: LCC PS8601.L41 N54 2019 | DDC C813/.6—dc23

Cover design by Rachel Cooper
Cover images: (field) Lynn Villalba / EyeEm / Getty Images;
(lattice) DmitriyRazinkov / Shutterstock

Printed and bound in Canada

10 9 8 7 6 5 4 3 2 1

Penguin
Random House
VIKING CANADA

for my family
y mi familia

Prologue

MANSOOR VISRAM WAKES TO a fluting sound, a distant melody like a muezzin's call. He half-opens his eyes. Dark fields extend to the horizon and merge seamlessly with the night sky. A perfect circle. The prairie hills are massive frozen waves. He feels something pecking at his feet. He lifts his head. A small domed shape bobs up and down at his feet, hammering at his icy body. The bird flies up and hovers over his chest. Her body is brilliant blue; her crown golden. Her breast is plump and glazed with rhinestone tassels instead of feathers. Mansoor is amazed that she can fly. He swipes the air and tries to catch her, but she flies up and out of reach. He plants his hands on the snow and struggles to stand, his veins a map of frozen rivers. The bird flies ahead of him and waits, like a siren willing him forward. A few steps and he falls to his knees. His clothes are an armour of ice. In the distance, the city lights are a pale smudge in the sky. He tries to stand again but his body jars, like a ship caught in icy waters. "Get up, Visram!" he orders himself. "Move!" Instead he falls, curls in the soft snow, and drifts off again. The bird lands on his shoulder. She nudges her way up to his ear and begins to sing.

PART ONE

Chapter 1

MANSOOR TRIES TO CLEAR the frost from the glass door of his store with a handkerchief. Instead, he creates a pattern of semicircles over the front sign, M.G. Visram & Son Dry Cleaners, Inc., Suiting Canada Since 1987. Outside, a thin, sharp snow is falling, the flurries visible only under the street lamps. It's past seven in the morning and still pitch dark. The winter sun will not rise for at least another hour. Most of the stores in the shopping plaza, located in an upscale neigh-bourhood in southwest Calgary, are closed: the travel agency, the hairdresser, the dentist's office, the video store. Only the dry cleaners and the twenty-four-hour convenience store are open, like fluorescent snow globes in the dark.

Mansoor turns around and inspects his store, just as he does each morning. It's a small space, only five hundred and fifty-three square feet, but it's well organized and this gives him a great deal of satisfaction. Gold frames pock the wall above the cash register, like a collage of family photographs. In one, a dollar bill, the first one he earned in Canada, from

August 1973. In another, his business licence, and yet another, his pledge to his customers. "I may not have the answer, but I will find it. I may not have the time, but I will make it." Against another wall, a short bookshelf holds his books with titles like *In Search of Excellence* and *Men's Strength & Power Training*, as well as biographies of men like Henry Ford, Bill Gates, and Neil Armstrong. The front of the store is separated from the back by a glass wall, allowing his customers to see what a well-organized operation he runs. Rows of suits and shirts, swathed in plastic, hang on a conveyor belt like headless men.

In the backroom, he flips open a calendar to an image of a lone Arctic wolf. A note under today's date, January 21, has been circled in red and starred. Banker, 3:30 p.m. Mansoor is ready. Fully prepared. He has been for months now. He needs the funds for a dry-cleaning plant, which is central to his new business plan. He has been waiting even longer to share his plan with his son, Ashif. He is the only one who will truly understand its enormity and significance in the marketplace. He is, after all, a brilliant businessman. Just like his father. Tomorrow, Mansoor will finally get his chance. Ashif is coming home for lunch when he is here from Toronto to attend important work meetings.

Above Mansoor's desk hangs a massive portrait of his father, a copy of the original photo that hung in all of their stores in Uganda, next to the image of Idi Amin, decreed by law, and one of the Imam, expected by the community. A trinity of men. In the photograph, his father stands proudly in front of his flagship store in Kampala. He is tall and rotund, his body weight proof of his wealth. He is in an ivory three-piece suit; a gold pocket watch, purchased in London, hangs from the vest pocket. His hands rest regally on top of a cane with a silver lion's head. High above him, the sign reads, Visram P. Govindji & Son, Established 1929.

When Ashif was a child, Mansoor found a magazine cut-out in the boy's desk with the face of Colonel Sanders wearing thick glasses and that silly beard. Underneath, scribbled in Ashif's babyish hand, he had written, "Dadabapa." Mansoor was furious. His father was a distinguished man, and here his son thought he was an American man who fried chicken? Mansoor immediately instituted Saturday morning classes for which he marched his son into his office for a lesson in family history. Ashif would clamber onto his father's office chair, his feet dangling high above the floor, as Mansoor told the story. "When your dadabapa arrived in Africa, he had nothing but two rupees to his name. Can you tell me how much that is?"

"Only enough to buy some bubblegum. But not the whole pack. Only one piece."

"Exactly!" He patted his son's shoulder. "Can you believe it? Your grandfather was a pauper from India. He was barely surviving—" he spun the globe on his desk and pointed at the state "—here in Gujarat. He worked in a quarry, toiling in the hot sun all day, breaking rocks, not to mention his back. And what for? To fill the coffers of other men." He banged a fist on the desk. "No, sir!"

Ashif banged his fist on the desk, too. "No, sir!"

"Dadabapa was thirteen years old—that's only seven years older than you, son—when he heard that many were building fortunes in Africa, men who were now owners of chain stores and underwriters to Arab, Indian, and Swahili entrepreneurs, whom stranded explorers came to for credit. Africa was their America. Dadabapa decided to take a chance. He saved enough money to buy a one-way ticket out of India and into the new world. He survived the wretched three-month *dhow* journey—the dysentery, the rats, and who knows what else—and arrived on the shores of Zanzibar in 1912. How long ago was that?" Lessons in math and science were always incorporated into each session.

Ashif reached for the calculator on his father's desk; Mansoor slid it away. "No cheating."

"Okay," Ashif giggled. He scrawled *sixty-five years* on his notebook.

"Yes, very good! But there were already too many young men with similar dreams and ideas. So what did your dadabapa do? He was very, very smart, you see. He moved inland to seek his fortune. A new frontier: Uganda. There, he apprenticed under an Indian store owner, trading his labour for a space to sleep on the roof of the store and one meal of *barazi* and *mumri*, beans in coconut milk and fried bread, served at noon each day. He learned to read and write in Hindi and Gujarati, to balance the books, to negotiate with vendors, to upsell customers. He also learned many new languages: Swahili, English, Kikuyu, and Buganda. He even picked up Japanese after World War II. Imagine! The Japanese were keen on rebuilding their country—good for them. They offered unbeatable quality and prices, making it essential to do business with them. Your grandfather traded his chisel for a pen, his *dhoti* for a business suit, and became a new man. In a matter of a few years, he changed the course of thousands of years of family history, like turning a steel ship with his bare hands."

Ashif bounced on his seat with excitement. "Just like Superman!"

"Yes, a real-life superhero. Fifteen years after he first set foot in Africa, at the age of twenty-eight, Dadabapa opened his own little dry goods shop in a small village called Tororo on the Ugandan-Kenyan border."

"Toronto?" Ashif asked.

"No," he laughed. "To-ro-ro. So close in name, yes. But worlds apart. This town wasn't even the size of your school. Imagine. Once he built up the business in Tororo, he followed the new European railroad across the nation and built a chain, opening new shops at each stop—Busembatia, Iganga, Jinja, and finally Kampala. A small empire. So you see, son, you can do anything. Be anyone you want. But you must never give up. Never! Understand?"

Ashif nodded.

"Mark my words, son. We were kings in Uganda, and we will be kings yet again in Canada."

"Me, too, Pappa?"

"Of course!" Mansoor lifted his son up into his arms. "One day everything is going to be yours."

Mansoor reaches for the stack of business plans on his desk. He sets two aside for his meeting with the banker, then takes another for his son. On it, he scribbles the initials *AMV*. Ashif M. Visram. There are so many things he wants to share with his son, not just his business plan. If only the boy would let him. He's not sure when the trouble began, but for some time now, Ashif has erected a wall between them. Whatever happened to change the boy? They used to tell each other everything. Now, when Ashif wants to tell him something, he tells his mother first, then she passes it on to him. What is she—his translator? But he wonders if pieces of information get lost in the exchange like in a game of telephone. He's not even sure she tells him everything. Maybe she's deliberately omitting parts of the message. But what bothers him more is the feeling that she is always between them. If it wasn't for her, he's sure they'd have the kind of relationship they had when Ashif was a child. When his son thought he was a hero, when he listened to what he had to say, laughed at his jokes, sought out his company. Ashif as a little boy, in his snowsuit and mukluks, running to him with open arms. This image emerges whenever he thinks of his son, even now. Like a parent who freeze frames the last time they saw a child they'd lost.

The idea for his new business came to him quite simply. He'd been searching for a way to grow his business, make his mark. Then on the day his car was at the shop, it struck him. He had to use public transportation, which he'd never used before, and that's when he noticed all the dead space in the LRT stations. There was a ticketing office, sometimes a convenience store, but that was it. Nothing else. No business would allow this kind of waste. But then, this was government. Inefficient fools. They had no regard for the bottom line. Why would they? It wasn't their money they were playing with. Not their name on the line.

What about a dry-cleaning kiosk? Commuters could drop off their cleaning on their way to work and pick it up on their way home. No one has time to waste, especially not busy professionals, and they are the ones who use dry-cleaning services the most. They need to look good all the time. He should know. It's why he opened his store here in Canyon Creek, a neighbourhood of young professionals. He's built his business by catering to them. They understand the value of excellence and are willing to pay for it. Mansoor's plan offers customers convenience; the city, a way to generate additional revenue; and him, a way to catapult his operation from one location to a chain of fifteen. A win-win for everyone.

To develop his plan, he conducted extensive market research over several months. He studied foot traffic patterns by station, and demographics by neighbourhood, along with his own reconnaissance missions. He spoke to commuters at train stations about their cleaning needs, their buying preferences. He surveyed the competition in each neighbourhood. He then compiled his data into spreadsheets (using Excel and PowerPoint, new tools he had learned through self-study) to create a cluster graph of the stations with the best potential. These stations formed the basis of his three-phase roll-out plan. Downtown Calgary, then affluent suburbs, and finally all others.

The key was centralized operations. A dry-cleaning plant that served all the locations. Business pundits called it vertical integration, but he didn't need a fancy term to understand the inherent sense of it. Instead of paying a supplier, Mansoor would become the supplier, allowing him to lower costs and maximize profits. He'd also take advantage of the latest technologies. A centralized computer system linking each kiosk to the plant via the Internet. Long-term, he imagined customers would even be able to check in their items and pay online. They called it e-commerce. Business was at the edge of a brave new world—unafraid of lightning-speed progress. If it was men like Edison and Bell who spurred the Industrial Revolution, now it was men like Steve Jobs, Bill Gates, and Sabeer Bhatia at the helm of the Digital Revolution. He shakes with excitement just thinking about it—he's going to be a part of it. This must be exactly how his father felt when he landed on the shores of Zanzibar. At the edge of a new frontier.

His plan is rock-solid, he knows that. The numbers speak for themselves. Now he needs to get in front of the right people at city hall. An arduous process. But it always is when you're dealing with the government. Here or in Uganda. The same layers of bureaucracy, like a set of gates that need to be pushed open before a bull is allowed into the arena.

Once he gets his foot in the door, he needs the city to see him as a serious player. Not as a one-man operation, a nobody, but as a big company that's capable of delivering on its business plan. When Federal Express started their operation, they played a recording of phones ringing, doorbells chiming, and crowds of people chatting in the background. Customers calling in were left with the impression that they were calling into a large company. Not a fly-by-night operation, but an organization they could trust. A plant will inspire the same confidence in the city. It will allow Mansoor to flex his muscles. Match power with power.

In the appendix of the plan, he's also included a Kiosk Operations Manual, a tool used in franchise operations, using his store as the model of high standards and efficiency. He will replicate his store, like a DNA strand, from one station to the next until the entire map of Calgary is covered. Then he'll expand beyond the city to Edmonton, Vancouver, Toronto, and Montreal. He sees his name light up across the country. M.G. Visram & Son, Suiting Canada Since 1987. Seen daily by hundreds of commuters. Thousands. Millions. "Then everyone will know my name!" He shoots an arm up in victory.

A man's laugh booms through the store.

Mansoor turns to see his father climbing out of the photograph's frame, as if it were a window, and into the store. The top of his head grazes the ceiling.

Mansoor steps back.

"Time's running out, boy," his father says, swinging his gold pocket watch back and forth. *Tick-tock, tick-tock.*

He feels the sting of his father's gaze. He casts his eyes down.

"How many times can I tell you, boy? A man cannot go out worse off than how he came in."

"Yes, sir."

"The future line of this family depends on you, boy. Your son's depending on you. You understand that?"

"Yes, sir."

"Twenty-five years in this country and *this* is all you've got to show for it?" Govindji crosses the store in one giant step. "A store the size of a closet? Pathetic."

"I can explain, Pappa . . ."

Govindji raises his hand. "No more excuses, boy. I've had it up to here with your excuses."

"I won't let you down. Not this time, Pappa. I promise."

Tick-tock, tick-tock.

"Are you sure?"

"Yes, sir, Pappa-Sir."

"How sure?" His father steps closer. Mansoor's heart races.

"One hundred and fifty percent sure. You can trust me."

Govindji whacks his cane across the back of Mansoor's calves. He groans, drops to his knees.

"Show me what you're made of, boy!" his father says.

Mansoor falls to the floor and starts a regimen of military push-ups. Up, down, clap. Up, down, clap.

His father taps his cane on the floor. "Faster, boy. There's no time to waste."

Mansoor struggles to keep up. Sweat pools under him.

His father presses a foot on his back. "Can you do it or not?"

Mansoor's legs shake, his arms, too. He can barely breathe. "I can ... do it, Pa ... ppa. I pro ... mise. I can."

The front doorbell jingles.

"Hello?" a woman's voice calls.

Mansoor collapses to the floor. He turns to see another figure. A customer at the cash counter. He struggles to stand. His legs are weak. His shirt is drenched. But when he gets to her, she's already out the door.

"I'm here!" he yells, following her outside but she won't stop.

Outside, his shirt stiffens instantly, like ice in a flash freezer. He rushes back inside. Customers! He shakes his head in frustration. One day, they are going to be the death of him.

Chapter 2

WHEN LAYLA WAKES, SHE finds a gold pocket watch that's been dismantled and laid out on the kitchen table in some sort of pattern, like a half-finished puzzle. The face, the hands, the springs and coils. A tiny screwdriver and hammer, too. Maybe the watch isn't working and Mansoor tried to fix it? She doesn't know. But she'll ask around or check the Ismaili phone directory to find someone who can fix it so that he won't have to.

Layla prefers Ismailis for all her activities—whether it's her seamstress (Habiba at Stitch-in-Time Alterations), her grocers (Sultan at Spice Village for her Indian and African goods and Poonjani at P.D. Wholesale Superstore for everything else), or her doctor (Dr. Jenny Kara at the local walk-in clinic). It isn't a just matter of supporting her community, which, of course, is very important, but it's also a matter of comfort—she doesn't have to stumble along and explain what she wants. They already know. Besides, it's a matter of budget. She receives a special discount at these establishments, just like everybody else in the community—depending on their negotiating skills. Try doing that at a regular store! Mansoor berates her for her attitude, for not "building bridges" with others. "Then what was the use of coming to this country?" he asks. But who said she wanted to come?

Layla cinches her apron tightly around her tiny waist, making it bellow out over her ample hips. She pins back her short, greying hair, then gets to work. She weaves through the house with an armful of Tupperware containers, setting them down on every available surface she can find. She starts in the kitchen with the counters, then the top of the microwave and a cart that holds onions and potatoes. Next, the dining room, where she works her way from the table and chairs to the hutch that holds her good dinnerware and glasses. Then, the living room with the deep freezer, the size of a coffin, pushed against a wall; the coffee table and side tables. She continues until every surface of her house is covered, not including the bathroom or the bedrooms, of course. A houseful of containers. A small factory for her home-cooking business that specializes in East African–Indian cuisine.

From her kitchen window, she spots her friends, Shamma and Almas, unmarried sisters who live in the townhouse across from hers. A light snow has settled on the walkways of the townhouse complex. In the dark, the tall, slim houses look like shadows that have been pulled up from the ground and erected to standing. Shamma sees her, too. She waves three fingers in the air. Layla balls her fist and rocks her arm up and down to indicate that she will join them for tea at three. She knows everyone in this complex and everyone knows her, not only because she goes to Headquarters Jamatkhana every day for evening prayers and, when she can, morning prayers, but also because she is well known by Ismailis throughout Calgary, and the country, for that matter, for her famous chicken samosas. Not that anyone has ever tasted them. That recipe is secret. It is reserved for the Imam only. The beloved Aga Khan.

The sisters look as if they're just starting their day, too, in their matching pink aprons and caps. They run a hair salon out of their basement. If Mansoor knew that she still goes to The Pink Comb, he would be livid. "They're running that business illegally, Layla. Just go to a regular salon, will you?" Besides, they are not just her friends. They are like family. They remind her of her sisters. Her mother, too. That's whom she misses the most. The company of women she loved, women she laughed with, women who knew everything about her. Without them, it feels as though pieces of her are missing.

When she told Shamma and Almas that Ashif was coming home, they asked her to bring him around for tea. She didn't have the heart to say no, so she said she would try her best.

They've known Ashif since he was a child; he even calls them *masi*, the formal name for a mother's sister. But there would be no time. He was only coming for lunch, even though he was going to be in Calgary for two nights before leaving for Vancouver for two more. Her heart broke when he gave her the news. She had not seen him for over a year now.

"At least come to jamatkhana with me on Wednesday? It's such a big night," she said, holding back her tears. "It's the Night of Power and everyone will be there." After all, praying on the Lailatul Qadr is equivalent to one thousand nights of prayer. It's the most powerful night of Ramadan, the month when Allah revealed the first chapters of the Koran to the Prophet.

"But I'm there for work, Mummy," Ashif said. "I'm booked from morning to night."

"Why don't you come after you finish in Vancouver on Friday? Stay with us for the weekend. We'll have so much fun."

"My flight is already booked back to Toronto. The company would never pay for the change fees. And they're an arm and a leg."

"Okay," she said, though she was not sure exactly what "arm and leg" meant. Her son speaks English with his father and a mix of English and Kutchi with her. Her English is good, but she often finds it difficult to follow what he says—not only because of the words he uses, but also because of his Canadian accent. As if he is from a different country, but of course he is not! She sometimes has to patch his words together. She agrees with him regardless of whether she understands him or not. But if he catches her, he berates her, tells her she has to learn to speak up. "It's a free country, Mummy! Just say what you want." She accepts his admonishments. Yet there are times when she wants to remind him that she is his mother.

"I want to come, Mummy," Ashif explained. "But I'm so busy. You know that."

"Yes, I know, *bheta*," she said, though she wasn't sure why her son is always so busy. She doesn't fully understand what he does for work. But she knows he has an important job at a big-big company.

Layla yearns to see her son's face, to hold him, the way she used to when he was a child. This is, she is sure, how all mothers separated from their children must feel, a constant sense of loss and longing. If only he had stayed here instead of moving so-so far away. "Calgary is better," she had urged when he told her his plan to stay in Toronto after finishing business school. "But all the big jobs are in Toronto. I have to stay."

His father agreed. "Just let him go in peace, will you, Layla? The boy is trying to make something of himself," he said, before giving his son a thumbs-up.

Back home, when someone moved to another town, it was only a short drive away. Or a ferry ride across Lake Victoria. But here, it is a completely different story. It takes nearly five hours on a plane from Calgary to Toronto. Five hours! Toronto might as well be in another country. She has, on more than one occasion, tried to measure this distance on the map that's still pinned to the wall of what used to be Ashif's bedroom but is now hers. How often she has walked her extended palm across Canada. Four palms long! Uganda is but an index finger, her hometown of Kisumu in Kenya not even the tip of a fingernail. Add in the different time zones, and you need to book an appointment, it seems, just to talk to someone in another city. Not that she has many people to call. Everyone she cares to know is here in Calgary. It is only her son who is not here. Her brothers are still in Kenya. Her mother, too. Her sister Shenaz in Australia. Her sister Gulnar in Pakistan. Her family spread across the globe like stars across the sky. She hasn't seen most of them in over twenty-five years. Not even before she left Uganda. There had been no time.

Only days before the deadline General Idi Amin set for Asians to get out of Uganda—November 8, 1972—Layla arrived with the baby at the Royal Air Force refugee camp sixty miles outside London. Months before, the Jewish community had already been thrown out. Then the Asians. Even the Muslims were given ninety days to get out. She had suggested to Mansoor that they could go stay with her family in Kenya. He refused to believe the decree and by the time he did, all countries surrounding Uganda had sealed their borders. "As if he'll throw us out. We were born in this country, for God's sake," he had said. At jamatkhana, many leaders echoed his view. But as each day passed, more stories of Amin's terror emerged: two men murdered as they filled their cars at a petrol station; a man thrown into a car boot and never seen again; twin sisters, students at Makerere University, kidnapped from their dorm room and gang-raped for days by army officers before one sister finally escaped, her nipples still bleeding when she was found on the side of a road. Panic spread. The community started to pack their bags. The United Nations organized airlifts out of the country. Each refugee was allowed to take one suitcase and £50. Layla smuggled out her wedding jewellery by sewing necklaces into Ashif's diaper, concealing earrings in his milk bottle, snapping bracelets around his tiny thighs. "At least you have a way out," Ashif's ayah, Rose, had said, wiping her eyes on the sleeve of her kanga. "What, Mamma, will the rest of us do?"

Layla had begged Mansoor to come with them. "Please, they will kill you." Mansoor refused. He wanted to stay as long as possible, to try and salvage their fortune. Besides, he reminded her, the British Consulate strongly advised against attempts to enter without proper documentation. Illegal entrants, they warned, would be detained indefinitely no matter if your wife and children were British subjects. It is terrible, they said, this expulsion of eighty thousand Asians, but we have no choice: we must stand by our voucher quota system. City councils, like Leicester's, placed adverts in Ugandan newspapers urging the Asians to stay away from their city. Layla countered Mansoor's refusal by naming other men who didn't have British passports but who were still going with their families. "I'm not like other men," he said matter-of-factly. "Be strong, Layla, for our son's sake. We'll be together again before you know it. I promise."

In London, she watched enviously as families clustered together at the camp cafeteria, eating and joking. Many of the illegal entrants were detained at the camps, but at least their families were together, and what else mattered? Eventually, many managed to immigrate successfully to countries like Sweden and

Argentina after applying to ads posted on the camp's bulletin board with the headline, "Have You Considered Emigrating?" Mansoor's three sisters and their families had been on the same flight to London, but she lost track of them in the crowd at Heathrow. When she tracked them down at another camp, they said they wished they could help her, maybe even move in together, but they were unable to leave—their husbands were detainees. Years later, she learned that their husbands had successfully smuggled their fortunes out of Uganda through a travel agent they knew. They had purchased airline tickets that went around and around the world, as if they were spooling the earth with miles of golden thread. Once they were released from the camps, they settled in Birmingham, where they quietly arranged for refunds.

At the camp, Layla was deeply lonely, the way she had been when she first moved from Kenya to Uganda to marry Mansoor. She didn't know anyone in Kampala. She hardly knew Mansoor, either. She'd only met him a few times before her father accepted his request for her hand in marriage. Layla never said anything, not even to her own family, about the agony of missing them. She kept her feelings to herself. She understood that a woman can't expect to be part of the same family she was born into. Her home, like her name, must inevitably shift to that of her husband's.

Months passed, and there was still no word from her husband, leaving her in a constant tangle of worry. Would she ever see him again? Was he still alive? In London, the Uganda Resettlement

Board began urging people to get jobs; newspapers reported that many refugees were getting too comfortable. Soon, representatives from different employers visited the camps and Layla was offered a job at a dressmaking plant in Manchester. The job included Council housing and child-minding facilities at the plant. But she didn't want anyone else to take care of her child, and she worried that Mansoor would not be able to find them if they left London. So she stayed put at the camp and prayed daily for his safe return to them. Each night, as she nursed the baby to sleep, she said the same thing to him, like a mantra. "Pappa will be back with us soon."

Chapter 3

ASHIF STANDS AT THE front of the executive boardroom
on the fifty-ninth floor of his company's Canadian head office
in downtown Toronto. The room is a wall of windows, like
a glass box suspended thousands of feet in the air. He has one
hand tucked into the pants pocket of his British-cut, single-
breasted, navy blue suit that fits his tall, slim body perfectly,
and the other rests on the podium next to him. He's clean-
shaven and his curly dark hair is smoothly combed back
with the exception of a small, stubborn curl that refuses to
cooperate despite the different products he used this morning, as he does every morning, to try to force it down.

At the back of the boardroom, on a skirted table, are several white carafes, a glass bowl filled with melting ice and a
few bottles of juice, and two silver platters, one with a lone
muffin. The executive team sits on plump, black leather chairs
around the oval boardroom table. Cups of coffee marked with
a soaring blue falcon, the company logo, sit in front of each of

them. They listen carefully, some taking copious notes, as Ashif explains his division's numbers.

He puts the next slide of his presentation, prepared by his assistant, on the overhead projector that's perched on a wheeled cart. A colourful chart filled with numbers appears on the white screen behind him. The chart is titled SALES FORECAST & BUDGET, and has labels like SALES VOLUME, PROFIT MARGIN, and GROWTH. The numbers are further broken down into years, quarters, and months. It's crucial to ensure period-over-period growth, a constant movement upward, like an endless escalator. That's what the company counts on, what shareholders expect, and what Ashif's job, like all sales jobs, is based on—delivering bigger and better numbers each and every quarter.

At the end of his presentation, the team congratulates him on a job well done and approves his budget. Rick beams in the background not only because Ashif achieved their goal, but also because he will, Ashif knows, get marks for mentoring and coaching him well—one of the eight key success factors that all senior managers and executives are tracked on for their performance reviews. Ken, the vice-president of finance, pats Ashif on his back. "Terrific presentation, kid. You're right on track." Glenda, the vice-president of marketing, shakes his hand firmly. "Nice work, Ash. We knew we made a good decision with you." She's the only woman on the executive team and is often dressed in pantsuits. "I bet she's got a pair of fucking balls under there, too," Rick had said in hushed tones to a group of men after she hit yet another home run at the annual company baseball tournament. Everyone laughed, Ashif included, even though he didn't find it funny.

Rick walks Ashif out. The executive lobby is a lush room with wood panelling, deep leather couches, and walls lined with perfectly hung portraits, like at a museum, of the company's past CEOs. Old white men in dark suits. Every single one.

"You ready for this week's meetings?"

"Absolutely," Ashif says.

"Of course you're ready. You always are." Rick pats Ashif on the back. "At this rate, you're going to be running this place, kid."

The company's laying off close to twenty thousand employees worldwide. Jobs are being made redundant as a result of the sales force being automated. All thanks to the Internet and e-commerce. Ashif has been chosen to lead the company's restructuring efforts for his division, starting first in Calgary and Vancouver. His job will be to convince targeted employees to take a layoff package. It's more cost effective than forcing a layoff, which sometimes prompts lawyers to get involved and ends up costing the company more. "It's one thing to be able to sell externally, but quite another to do it internally. That's the mark of a true salesman," Rick had said when he gave Ashif the news of his appointment. It's a test like the many tests he has passed before. How well he does will determine if he'll continue on the mid-management track or if his career path will be catapulted to the executive track—the fast track, as his co-workers called it, the goal of every new recruit hired by the company, including Ashif. He had confidently proclaimed that this, too, was what he wanted during each of the five interviews he'd had with progressively more senior managers that it took to land the job. The year he graduated from business school, the company hired one person. He was it.

The executive track is clearly mapped out. It has a separate route and leads to the top of the company's organizational chart. The chart is divided into trading regions and sub-regions, each territory in the world clearly marked and managed. Level IV means access to what everyone at the company refers to as the Golden Room. Level IV managers receive stock options, increased expense accounts (particularly for entertaining clients), business class travel (and, if available, access to the company jet), membership to the Granite Club, and comprehensive health benefits. "With great power comes the golden handcuffs, Spidey, not freedom," colleagues joked. "Once you're in that room, they own you."

In the lobby, Rick taps a card on a security panel and the glass doors swing open. "Good luck this week."

As Ashif walks through the doors, he sees a faint reflection of himself in the glass, as if there's another man trapped inside. He takes the elevator down to the twenty-sixth floor, where he weaves through a maze of cubicles, filled with administrative staff and junior salespeople, to his office in the northwest corner. His assistant, Patty, stands up from her desk and greets him with a stack of messages.

"Anything urgent?" he asks as he walks into his office.

"Just one." She follows behind in small steps, her red pencil skirt and heels restricting her. "Serge needs to speak to you about the meetings in Atlanta next week."

"Okay. Get him on the line for me." Ashif sets a massive binder with the company's restructuring plans down on his desk. He sits down, rolling his high-back leather chair to his desk. In the building across the street, small, dark figures move behind the square windows like birds in glass cages.

She hands him an envelope labelled FAIRMONT HOTELS & SPAS on the front. "For your mom."

"Thanks." He's sure Patty thinks he's a mamma's boy. Nothing could be further from the truth.

"I'm sure she'll love it."

"Hopefully," he says, though he's never sure what his mother likes or wants. She never tells him anything directly. She speaks in code so that even when he was a child, if his father asked her if she wanted to go for ice cream and she answered, "Only if Ashif does," he knew that meant yes. But his interpretations weren't always right. He finds himself constantly worrying about her, even now when she's thousands of miles away. As if she's always with him, stuck to him like a foot on wet tar.

Patty tells him she's confirmed his hotel reservations. Two nights in Calgary, then on to Vancouver for two more. His limo to and from the airport are also confirmed.

"Can you tell the limo company that there will be two stops in Calgary?" he instructs Patty. "I'm going to have lunch with my parents before I head to the hotel." He writes down an address and hands it to her. "My parents' home," he says, though his parents would both admonish him if they heard him call it their home. In their minds, their home was his home in the same way that they thought his home was theirs. There was no difference between *mine* and *yours*. As if everything belonged to the family. If you believed anything else, you would be considered selfish.

"That's so nice," Patty says, as she scribbles on her notepad. "You're a good son, Ash."

When she leaves, he unlocks the top drawer in his desk, lifts the pen tray, and retrieves a bottle. In the distance, he can see an army of headlights moving down Bay Street. In the evening, he'll watch the same stream in reverse when people return home, leaving behind office towers, like empty shells, with only the janitors and a few others, like him, at their desks. He taps a small white pill from the bottle. It's tiny but he can't manage without it. His doctor agrees. Ashif has been on anti-depressants for years now. He presses the pill to the back of his throat and swallows.

Chapter 4

MANSOOR PULLS INTO A shopping plaza, not far from his store, for his appointment with the bank. He closed the dry cleaners for an hour, putting a sign up on the front door to tell customers he would be back at 4:30 p.m., ample time for the banker to review his mortgage application. He gathers his things and steps out. A briefcase and an accordion file with all his papers. The store's financial records, his tax returns (personal and business), the deed to his home. Ten years' worth of numbers. But that's how it is with bankers. You have to prove yourself, as you do in a court of law, except at a bank you are guilty until proven innocent. But he's not worried. His store has a solid track record and he has the numbers to prove it. He's also brought along three property listings from his real estate agent, although there's only one he's really interested in. An abandoned storage facility on the outskirts of Calgary.

Outside, the sky is an endless patch of white and blue. The parking lot is a mess of snow and mud. As Mansoor crosses it, a man in torn clothes and long, knotted hair steps out from behind a Dumpster. He reeks of urine. Mansoor steps back, startled.

"Spare some change?" the man asks.

Mansoor hesitates, then he remembers Uganda.

Days after Idi Amin's deadline to leave expired, Mansoor boarded one of the last U.N. charter flights out of Uganda. He found his seat through a haze of cigarette smoke. The flight was packed with stateless Asian men, men who now belonged nowhere.

Soon after Layla and Ashif left for England, five army officers had stormed into one of his shops, brandishing machetes. They demanded money and the keys. Mansoor wanted to resist, but he was overcome with an intense fear. It was as if he were leisurely swimming at the Aga Khan Sports Club when he suddenly realized that he wasn't in the pool, but in Lake Victoria. Bulging crocodile eyes surfaced all around him. He complied with the officers and quietly walked out of Visram P. Govindji & Son, Inc.

He'd rushed home through the city's back streets and packed within minutes. He then drove to the gurdwara with his house servant, Joseph, in the passenger seat. The Sikh temple was now the only safe haven for people who hadn't been able to get out before Amin's deadline. At the temple, Mansoor removed his suitcase from the trunk, then gave Joseph the keys to his Mercedes and the family house, too.

The plane taxied down the runway and soon they were airborne. A few men became boisterous, yelling slurs out to Amin, "Good riddance, General Dodo." Some, though, were certain he'd rescind his policy and ask them to come back. Not that they knew where they were going. Others spoke to each other in whispers, but most, like Mansoor, sat quietly in their seats and stared out their windows. In the distance, Mansoor could see the vast blue of Lake Victoria and below him, the city of Entebbe. Though Kampala was too far in the distance, in his mind's eye, he could see the houses where he had lived as a child, each one larger than the last as his father continued to expand his empire. He could see the jamatkhana on Jinja Road where he played in the garden courtyard as a child; the primary school that he used to walk to with his friends early each morning, carrying his lunch of chapati and dhal curry; the years in secondary school with that same group of friends; the countryside where the family picnicked each Sunday, roasting sticks of spicy mishkaki on an open fire; his father's first store on Martin Road, opened in 1929, and which he was allowed to manage by himself when he turned sixteen. He could see the Aga Khan Hospital where Ashif was born; City Bar where he celebrated the birth with a roomful of men; the Ismailia Cemetery where his father was buried. Soon, Uganda vanished under a screen of white clouds.

Fourteen hours later, they landed in Vienna, where they were cleared through a special line at immigration then escorted into the arrivals hall to throngs of cheering Austrians. Some held up signs. *Willkommen Refugees!* Others reached out to shake their hands as though they were film stars. One woman gifted Mansoor a sandwich and a bag of chocolate coins. "We are very much sorry for your pain, sir," she said. He didn't want it, but he understood. She was only trying to welcome him to her country. He took the food and thanked her, though her gesture made him feel small. As if he was a beggar. Passing through the revolving door from customs into the arrivals hall had spun him back in time. He was exactly where his father had been when he landed on the shores of Zanzibar sixty years ago. A pauper with nothing to his name.

At the refugee camp in Austria, it soon became clear that only so many countries would take them. So many countries, like America, had turned their backs to the refugees, but not Canada. Pierre Elliott Trudeau generously opened the country's borders to Uganda's Asians, including the Ismailis. If it wasn't for the prime minister, Mansoor doesn't know what would have become of them.

At the time of Uganda's independence, the British had promised to protect those who were worried about a fever of excessive African nationalism; they encouraged people to maintain their British passports. But without Ugandan citizenship, the new African government would not allow Asians to operate their businesses. So, what to do? Stay in the safe middle. Stuck in the middle, more like it. Let the wife maintain a British passport and the husband can get a Ugandan passport.

What bloody irony: Amin threw them out because Asians had split loyalties. Why hadn't they chosen to become Ugandan citizens at the most critical time in the country's history? *You have milked the cow, but you did not feed it.* Some said that Amin threw them out because an Asian family refused him their daughter's hand in marriage. Then the Queen refused entry to those without passports even if their families had already been airlifted to London.

During one of their history lessons, he told Ashif that the prime minister had rescued him by pirouetting into the Vienna refugee camp in a red cape and beret with a maple leaf on it before he scooped him up and away like a superhero. *Merci beaucoup, Monsieur Trudeau. Merci beaucoup.* Since becoming a Canadian citizen, Mansoor insisted that he and Layla vote Liberal; she did (he hoped) even though she said there was no point in voting, especially during provincial elections. What difference could they make? There had been no change to Alberta's Conservatives in decades. She may have been right, but that was hardly the point. Why couldn't she understand such a simple matter?

Mansoor fishes out a ten-dollar bill from his wallet and hands it to the homeless man.

The man kisses it and raises it to the sky. "Thank you, sir!"

"Good luck to you," Mansoor says, feeling a deep sense of pride and dignity as he steps through the bank's doors. He is now the host, here in this great new country of his.

The banker, Jon Brady, is younger than Mansoor expected. He looks about Ashif's age and that pleases him. He doesn't want some stodgy old banker who might have a hard time understanding new technologies and his groundbreaking business plan. Mansoor places a copy of his business plan, like a menu, in front of Jon. The banker sits back and scribbles notes on the business plan as Mansoor speaks with great enthusiasm about break-even point, sales volume, the Internet, and e-commerce. When he's done, Jon praises him.

"You've got a terrific plan here. Very innovative."

Mansoor laughs. See! He knew this would be easy. His plan is rock-solid.

"My main concern though is that your debt service ratio is a little high," Jon says.

That makes no sense to Mansoor. "But I have no debt. None! I paid off the gas station debt years ago. I've even paid off my house. I have a clean slate."

"Yes, I can see that from your records." He lightly taps his pen against his knee.

"I never missed a payment. I was never late. Not even once." Mansoor feels as if the banker is trying to convict him of something even though he is innocent.

"Yes, I understand, Mansoor. But the debt service coverage ratio is connected to income, as you know. Your current income can support the payments, but from our perspective there's just not enough breathing room if your income goes down."

"My income won't go down! It will only go up now that I'm expanding." He fumbles with his business plan and opens it up to a graph. "See that!" He traces the income line from 1987 to 1997, his finger like a gondola climbing a ski hill.

"Unfortunately, we don't lend based on projections. We need something more solid. It would help your case if you could secure your contract with the city first."

"I can't secure the contract without the plant, Jon."

"Right. It's a bit of a chicken-and-egg story, then. Sorry, that happens sometimes."

Mansoor digs his fingers into his knees. "But I've done business here for twenty-five years. The bank knows me. Doesn't that count for anything?"

"It counts for a lot. We truly appreciate your business. I just don't have any wiggle room here. These are the bank's rules."

Mansoor glimpses the framed certificate on Jon's wall. Mount Royal College, Business. Is that all the education this boy has? No wonder. His bosses will be so angry if they find out how they treated him, let such a solid opportunity slip out of their hands. "My son went to business school at the University of Toronto. One of Canada's top, but I'm sure you know that."

"It's a tough school to get into," Jon says. "You must be proud."

"Yes, very." Mansoor's chest swells. "My son got top marks, even won a scholarship, all expenses paid. Secured a top-rate job, too, of course." Meanwhile, Mansoor has to listen to this lowly banker who claims to have a degree in business. "Can I speak to your manager?"

"I am the manager," Jon says.

Mansoor is dumbfounded. What kind of operation is this? They'll give a job to anyone who walks in off the street.

"Look, Mansoor," Jon continues, "you do have other options. You could consider a B lender. Companies like Abrahams & Abrahams. They'll take on higher levels of risk."

Mansoor just nods. But he's no risk! He would never use a B lender. Their interest rates are ridiculous. Might as well go to a loan shark.

"How about a partner, Mansoor? Even a silent one. Someone who could act as your guarantor. That would give the bank the extra assurance it needs. Do you have anyone who could do that for you?"

Mansoor shakes his head. "I have no one."

Tick-tock. Tick-tock. Tick-tock.

Jon hands the business plan and loan forms back to him. "If your circumstances change, please come back to us. We'd be happy to help you." Jon then stands up and extends his hand to Mansoor. "Thank you for coming in."

Mansoor's legs tremble as he walks down the long hallway from Jon's office to the front of the bank. He hears heavy footsteps behind him. He turns to see his father approaching. His heart races. He quickens his pace. So does his father.

"I knew you couldn't do it!" his father says. His words

pound down the hallway, like waves through a narrow channel. "You're useless. Utterly useless."

That's all Mansoor can hear. He's drowning in his father's words. Drowning in shame.

He doesn't realize what has happened until he is on the ground.

"Are you okay?" a voice asks.

Mansoor turns to see a security guard kneeling next to him. Then, a wall of glass in front of him. Outside, a parking lot of cars and snow. On the floor next to him, the scattered contents of his briefcase. He touches his forehead as if he's expecting blood. But there isn't any. Just a throbbing pain.

The security guard tries to help him up.

"No, no. I'm fine . . . fine." He presses a hand to the glass and raises himself up.

Mansoor stares at the mess of papers on the ground. At the top, his business plan with the initials, AMV. That's when it comes to him: Ashif! Of course. He can co-sign the loan for him. He has a solid job at a blue-chip company—and he's doing so well there. He's my son, isn't he? He laughs out loud in relief. Normally, he would never burden his son with a financial matter. He was the head of the household, not Ashif. But he wasn't asking his son for money. Of course not! He would never do that. He just needs his signature, that's all. And who better to vouch for him than his own son? Mansoor's shoulders begin to soften, his mind, too. He can finally relax. His son will be here soon and then everything will be fine.

Chapter 5

LAYLA'S APRON IS STAINED with a day's worth of cooking. The kitchen counters are dusted with flour, the hood fan is set on high, and all six elements on her stove are in use. On one of them, a bowl made of tinfoil lined with perfume-soaked sugar. It helps her fumigate the house. "Once you let those spices settle in, they are impossible to remove," Mansoor always says. It's the same reason he asks her to keep his clothes sheathed in dry-cleaner's plastic. Otherwise, he says, his customers might run away. She doesn't like it, but she understands. She knows white people don't like food that is too spicy. Not that she has ever eaten at any of their houses, but she's eaten at a few restaurants here to know.

When Ashif was growing up, Mansoor insisted they celebrate birthdays at a restaurant. White Spot. Ponderosa. Chuck E. Cheese. He wanted his son to do what Canadian children did. She relented, arming herself with a bottle of mircha chili in her purse. But when she doused her food with it, Ashif made her stop. "God, Mummy!" he whispered harshly. "People are watching." Mansoor agreed. He asked her to put the bottle away and she did. After that, she kept her mircha bottle at home and learned how to force the bland food down on its own.

Layla lifts a heavy pot from the stove and shuffles to the counter, where she carefully sets it down. Scents of coconut and coriander rise from the *kuku paka*. She ladles the coconut curry, chicken, and eggs into the rows of Tupperware containers, stopping occasionally to shake her hands loose from the stiffness. She lets the steam escape, then snaps the lids on, running her finger around the outer edge to make sure each one is tightly sealed. She continues with the rest of the dishes on tonight's menu then stacks each completed order into a plastic bag pre-labelled with the customer's name. Meals that many won't eat until they break their fast after sundown. Layla is fasting for the month of Ramadan, too. People fast for different reasons, but for her, it is a symbol of her dedication to the Imam.

When she is finally done with her orders, she sits down at the kitchen table with a cup of tea and reviews the elaborate menu for Ashif's luncheon. It's been so long since she has had a chance to cook for him and she does not want to skimp on a thing. The main dishes will include masala tilapia with thick-cut chips, Kenyan-style chicken biryani, and spinach curry served with *rotli* bread. For appetizers, *dhorka*, a semolina cake, with tamarind-date chutney, fried sticks of *mogo*-cassava, and potato-*champs* with green-chili chutney. She will end the meal with *faloodha*—a milky pudding—and sweet meats. She knows she is making too much, but she would rather have more than less. It was guiding principle every time she hosted. She loved entertaining. So did Mansoor. But that was so long ago. They haven't entertained for years now.

Layla pushed open the swinging door to her kitchen, holding a flute of passion fruit juice and sparkling water. Her hair was in an updo and she was dressed in an Audrey Hepburn–style dress, a gift from Mansoor, who insisted she buy something new for every celebration—from Eid to New Year's. This time it was for their third wedding anniversary. She'd special-ordered this dress from Dubai. The kitchen buzzed with African staff, some of whom were hired for the party. They were in smart white coats and carried trays of steaming kebabs and crushed-ice cocktails.

"Mary, Mary, where are you?" she called out in Swahili.

On the radio, a news announcer read out the headlines, "General Idi Amin Dada visited Kampala University to attend a massive rally in support of our great new leader."

"Yes, Mamma?" Mary asked, making her way to Layla.

"Is the cake ready?"

"Yes, everything is ready, Mamma." She pointed to a trolley with a three-tiered white cake decorated with jasmine and rose petals, a replica of their wedding cake. A ribboned knife rested next to it.

"Okay, good. Please bring it out in half an hour."

"Yes, Mamma."

"And please turn off the radio. It's noisy enough in here as it is."

"Yes, Mamma."

Layla weaved through the house, past her guests dressed in smart cocktail attire—all of them Indian, many of them Ismaili—past walls pocked with family portraits and Mansoor's athletic trophies, to the garden where a band was playing a marimba song. Guests were dancing, and she knew exactly where she would find her husband.

Mansoor stood at the centre of a group of friends. He was in an Italian-cut, dark blue suit, which he'd bought in London for their wedding and only wore at their anniversary parties. With it, he wore a red silk scarf tucked into the jacket pocket and metal-tipped shoes. He still looked so dapper in it. As she walked to him, she remembered the first time she met him, a formal introduction brokered by her mother in Kisumu and Mansoor's aunt in Kampala, a ferry ride across Lake Victoria. Layla's family was poor, but she still garnered many suitors. She was known for her beauty, her cooking skills, and her family's reputation as upstanding members of the community. Mansoor was known for his charm, his intelligence, and his family's wealth. He would, her father was confident, give his daughter a life his salary never could. Mansoor wasn't especially handsome, but he was tall and strong, and Layla could see the outline of his muscular arms through his muslin shirt. With him, she felt nothing would go wrong. Three months later, they were married. Their wedding night was the first time they kissed. The first time any boy had touched her.

Layla reached for her husband's elbow to indicate she was back; he stepped aside to make room for her. Rose, Ashif's ayah, brought the baby to her, just as she had asked her to. Ashif was a few weeks old and many of their friends had yet to see him.

"Look who's come for dinner," Layla said, pulling back his blanket.

The women leaned in, oohing and ahhhing. Bilkis, a neighbour in a gold silk sari, tapped the baby's cheek, as if testing a fruit for ripeness. "Such a sweetie, he is."

"*Mumbarki* to you!" Tariq, Mansoor's friend and golfing partner, shook Mansoor's hand. "Is he ready to take over the business yet?"

"Soon, very soon," Mansoor said, raising his whisky glass.

"Aye, don't encourage him, Tariq *Bhai*," Layla said. "He'd have my son at one of his stores by tomorrow if he could."

The group laughed.

"So, when's the stork bringing the next one, Visram?" another friend asked.

"Soon, if I have it my way," Mansoor said with a wink.

"Poor you," Bilkis whispered in Layla's ear. "You went through so much with this pregnancy as it was."

Layla nodded. Her labour had been twenty-four hours long. The baby refused to come. "A bit shy, that's all," the doctor said reassuringly. "We'll just have to coax him out into the world," the nurse added as she wheeled Layla to the operating room for an emergency C-section. But when Layla held the baby in her arms, her happiness was pure and full. She decided then that she wanted a big family and when she told Mansoor, he heartily agreed. It was, he said, what he had always wanted, too.

"Should I feed him, Mamma?" Rose reached for the baby.

"No, no. I want to." Layla folded the baby back into his blanket. "I'll be back soon," she announced to her guests.

"Take your time," Mansoor replied, and she could see the glow of pride and admiration in his eyes.

As she nursed Ashif in her bedroom, she felt a deep sense of comfort and joy. Here in her home, with her husband, the murmur of their friends downstairs, the weight of her child in her arms. She never imagined that their lives could be so easily uprooted. In a blink of an eye. Idi Amin's expulsion order was just months away.

The doorbell rings. It's her neighbour, Ramzan. He delivers her orders to her customers and they pay him directly. Under his down-filled jacket, he's in an undershirt, his necklace visible, a tiger-eye gold chain that his girlfriend, a Turkish woman, gave him. "To keep the evil eye away," he explained to Layla. "You know, with my good looks, she can't be too careful," he joked.

When he's finished loading the orders into his car, she gives him an extra container of chicken pilau for himself, not that she charges him. He doesn't charge her for the personal rides he gives her either. Ramzan runs multiple businesses. Besides delivering her orders, he sells knock-off handbags and perfumes from a street cart, and he runs a private taxi service for women in the neighbourhood who don't drive or don't have cars.

"Thank you. Smells delicious as always, *Bai*," he says. "I'm taking some of the ladies shopping tomorrow morning. Big sale at Sears. Want to come?"

She hesitates but thinks better of it. With the continued increase in orders, she can afford a new dress. When she started her business, most of her customers ordered only for big occasions like Eid or when relatives were coming, but now more and more families were on a daily schedule—mostly the youths, who nowadays hired people do everything in their house: cooking, cleaning, mowing, shovelling, fixing-bixing. Just like back home. But who knew that one day she would be the servant?

"Yes, why not?" she says. She hasn't gone shopping for such a long time and she wants to look nice for Ashif.

"Good-good. See you in the morning, *Bai*."

In the pantry, Layla pulls out a tiffin box tucked in with her spices. A makeshift cash register she uses for her business. One compartment has cash, the other, expense receipts, and the last, her tithe. She submits the first two to Mansoor each week when he does the accounts. The third is her secret. "Charity begins at home, Layla," she can hear him say if he ever found out. But *dasond* isn't charity. It is her duty as a *momin*. She counts out fifty dollars from the customer compartment and tucks it into her apron pocket. What you give always comes back tenfold. This is *barakat*. The secret of life.

Chapter 6

WHEN ASHIF COMES HOME from work, he finds Caity waiting for him in the lobby of his condo building. She's in yoga gear and her long blonde hair is tied back in a ponytail. He met her at his gym and they've been dating for a couple of months. Though he made it clear to her right from the beginning that he's not interested in a relationship. He didn't say it, but he doesn't want to be tied down. Even thinking about it makes him feel claustrophobic. Caity agreed. That's all she wants, too. But after last weekend, he's not so sure. She needed a date to a wedding, and he reluctantly agreed to go.

During the dinner reception, the table toasted Caity's recent call to the bar and she told them about Ashif's possible promotion—how he was pegged as the guy to nail it. Everyone then raised their glasses for him. A woman added that they made a beautiful couple. Another guest told Caity she'd look stunning in a wedding sari. Her husband agreed and joked that they wanted an invitation to their wedding. They'd never been to an Indian wedding before and had heard how lavish they were. Caity played along and so did he, but what bothered him was how much she seemed to enjoy it. It also bothered him that people assumed that he was Indian. Not that he said anything. He never does. It's just easier. Like an olive branch that saves him from explaining his roots.

India-Africa-Muslim. He doesn't fit into any category easily. He looks Indian but he isn't. He was born in Africa but isn't African. He's Muslim but not *that* kind of Muslim. Saying anything would only lead to endless questions, as if he was an expert, a guide at a museum. But he hardly knows enough about Ismailism, let alone Islam. He wouldn't be able to discuss his family's history, either. All he knows is that his mother is from Kenya and his father is from Uganda. He has no idea which city either was born in, though he knows he was born in Kampala. It says so on his passport. He was just a baby when they left and there are no pictures of him from there. None of his parents, either. As if they never existed until they arrived in Canada, which is fine by him. He has never been back and has no desire to go, either. Uganda has nothing to do with him. He is Canadian. Not that people always accept that when they ask him where he's from. No, but where are you really from? As if they are border guards and he's trying to enter the country illegally. It leaves him feeling that he doesn't belong here. But he doesn't belong anywhere else, either. He's perpetually in limbo. No man's land.

"What are you doing here?" Ashif asks, kissing Caity hello.

"Our date," she says, lifting a paper bag from the floor. "I brought groceries for us to cook together. Did you forget?"

"Sorry, I did," he says.

"Want to reschedule?" she asks.

He's exhausted and still needs to pack for his trip. It's already eight. But he feels bad that he'd forgotten and kept her waiting. "No. Let's go up."

Ashif's condo isn't luxurious, but it's close to work and has everything he needs. Not that any of the things are his. The furniture, the artwork, the dishware. Nothing except his clothes and personal items. Like he's living in a hotel. He can check out anytime he wants.

After dinner and sex, Caity leaves, and he's relieved to have his place back to himself. He can breathe again. He powers on his desktop and settles into his evening routine. The computer whirs, taking a few minutes to turn on. Meanwhile, he makes himself a gin and tonic. He knows he's not supposed to drink while he's on anti-depressants. But it's only one drink. Maximum two. He looks forward to it, like his reward at the end of a long day. He clicks open a file called "Mummy." The spreadsheet tracks his salary, his expenses, his investments. He's asked his broker to put all his money into safe instruments. GICs, bonds, T-Bills. Some stocks. He doesn't want to take any risks. Not until he's got enough money to leave his job. For years now, Ashif has been saving his money with one goal in mind: his mother. She's already fifty-four, and he wants her to stop working and start enjoying her life.

He's saving enough for both his parents to retire. His mother won't stop working unless his father does, too. The retirement plan includes all their monthly expenses including luxuries, health insurance to supplement Alberta's health care, yearly vacations and visits abroad to see family, and a trade up from their house to a condo. A good life. If he stays on track at the company, he'll have enough in ten years. He'll be close to forty. His mother, sixty-five. He traces a finger to the top of the line graph, 2008. That's when he'll get out. Like a prison sentence. But he knows he can do it. He has to. Then, he'll finally be free to do whatever he wants.

Al-Karim asked Ashif if he wanted to go to the Ismaili career fair with him. He didn't. Al-Karim said, neither did he. But he reminded him of the real reason they should go: hot girls.

Al-Karim was a visa student from Nairobi studying Hotel and Restaurant Management at a local college. He was a star athlete and voted MVP at the Ismaili Triangular Games the last three years running. The girls loved him and the guys admired him, too. Ashif was fifteen but had never kissed a girl, never even held a girl's hand yet. He was too skinny, too shy. Not the kind of guy girls noticed.

"Good, take him," his mother said to Al-Karim. She approved of any Ismaili event he wanted to go to and anything with Al-Karim. He had a beat-up old Datsun and helped her with their errands—grocery shopping, fixing things around the house, rides to jamatkhana. Ashif was still a year away from getting his driver's licence and even if he had it, it wouldn't do any good. The family car was with his father in Rocky Mountain House. He'd moved there over three years ago to take care of the family business, a gas station and convenience store. He only came home on Sundays for dinner. But it was never enough time and Ashif missed him constantly.

The career fair was packed, mostly with teenagers. Booths circled the gymnasium showcasing careers like medicine, engineering, law, business, and teacher education. At the registration desk, students could sign up for tutorial help or workshops like "The Art of Building Your Resumé."

Al-Karim pointed to the tutorial list, "Arzeen Dawood, chemistry, biology, calculus." "You know her, right?"

Ashif nodded. Of course he knew her. Everyone knew Arzeen. She had huge doe eyes and perfectly straight hair dyed caramel-blonde. She was beautiful. Not that Arzeen had any idea who he was. Why would she?

That's when Al-Karim revealed his plot. He needed Ashif to keep her little sister, Shafina, company while he took Arzeen for a drive. "Her old man will have my head if he finds out."

Ashif agreed even though he was nervous. He had a hard

time speaking to people, let alone a beautiful girl. But he didn't want to lose his chance to meet Arzeen's sister. He reminded himself of his father's advice about meeting new people. Make a joke, smile, people always like a friendly face.

"Excellent, man. Thank you." Al-Karim pointed to the bleachers. "There's your girl."

Ashif turned to see a girl sitting at the top with a massive book splayed open on her lap. She had thick glasses and a navy-coloured beret over a mass of curly hair. She wore a tartan skirt, fishnet stockings, and army boots. "Her?" he asked incredulously.

"Sorry, man. She's a bit of a freak, I know." Al-Karim laughed. "Hard to believe she's related to Arzeen, right?"

"I don't know, Al-Karim . . ." he said, trying to back out of their deal. If he hangs out with a girl like her, everyone will think he's a weirdo, too. He doesn't want to stand out, be called names as he was when he was younger. He was often teased for being too small by other kids. And at school, for being brown, too. The first time it happened, he didn't even know what it meant. He was six and a new friend told him he wasn't allowed to play with them anymore because he was a Paki. Ashif thought it was in reference to his lunches, which his mother always overpacked. But when he told his mother, she explained the real meaning and told him it didn't matter. That boy wouldn't have been a good friend, anyway. Ashif asked her not to pack his lunches with Indian food anymore and she agreed.

"Next time I'll set you up with someone beautiful, okay? You just need a little more muscle, man." Al-Karim squeezed his biceps. "That's what all the babes want."

"But what am I going to talk to her about?" Ashif asked.

Al-Karim picked up a flier from the registration desk and handed it to him. "Start with this." The title read, TOP 10 CAREER CHOICES OF 1986. SPONSORED BY THE ISMAILI ECONOMIC DEVELOPMENT COMMITTEE. "About time the two of you started thinking about your future, don't you think?" he said with a laugh.

Ashif plodded up the bleachers to Shafina and handed her the flyer.

She glanced up from her book. "For me?" Under her thick glasses, her eyes were large and bulbous.

"Yup." He plopped himself next to her.

"Are you with the Ismaili Students' Association or something?"

"Nope. A friend asked me to hand them out." He planted his elbows on his knees and cupped his face.

She scanned the form and handed it back. "Thanks, but I'm not interested in propaganda."

"Propaganda?" he said, sitting up. "This isn't propaganda." He nervously scanned the gym. Everyone could see them up here.

"It is when it only gives you one side of the story. Besides, I don't need a workshop," she said using air quotes for the word *workshop*, "to tell *me* what to do. Please, people. I already know what I want to do."

"Really?" he asked, surprised by her confidence.

"Yup. Liberal Arts." She licked a finger and turned to the next page in her book. "Well, for my first degree, anyway."

The word *arts* felt foreign to him, reserved for rich white kids, like skiing and cottage vacations. "But what can you do with an arts degree?"

"I don't know." She pushed her glasses back up. "But I'll figure it out. I want to explore the possibilities and then I'll decide. I mean, that's the key to a good education, right? To broaden our minds and learn about the world. It can't just be about making lots of money. What about you? What are you going to do?"

He shrugged. He'd never considered entering a program without first knowing what he'd do after graduation. It was important to have an endgame in mind. Know how you're going to make a living before wasting money on a degree. That's what everyone—especially his father—seemed to say. He was leaning toward something like chartered accounting or maybe pharmacy. He was good at math and chemistry, even if he didn't like them. Shafina's ideas seemed both ludicrous and liberating. "Do your parents know about this?" he asked.

She laughed. "*They* don't need to know *everything* about my life. They'll find out soon enough, anyway," she said, her face turning grim. "Larkin was right. You have to leave home as soon as you can. Before your parents screw you up."

Who's Larkin? he wanted to ask but didn't. He was entranced by the way she spoke. Her words flowed out of her with such strength but softness, too. Like gold, melting. It took him a few seconds to respond and even then, all he could muster was, "Oh, that's interesting."

"Not like there's anything they can do about it, anyway. I'm just going to get a scholarship and get out of here. Do what I want to do."

He could hardly grasp her meaning. As if she was speaking a foreign language. Doing what she wanted without the approval of her parents was crazy. He would never do that to his parents. "What university do you want to go to?"

"It's not just about the school. I want to be in the right city, you know. Montreal, New York, Paris, Cairo." She adjusted her beret. "Calgary is so . . ." she rolled her eyes, "pedestrian. Who wants to live among cowboys? I want to be a moth, not a candle."

Her words continued to confuse him, but he liked the sound of them. The rhythm. "What does that mean . . . I want to be a moth, not a candle?"

"Poets! I want to live among poets," she said, raising her eyebrows. "You know, like Rumi. *Don't pretend to be a candle, be a moth.*" She lifted her book and turned the cover to face him. *Divan-e-Shams-e-Tabrizi*, by Jalaludin Rumi. "You know him, right? He's like, famous. Well, maybe not here and definitely not with those heathens," she said pointing to the crowd.

Ashif shrugged. He felt that he didn't know anything. He hadn't even heard of this guy, let alone read him. All the books on the required reading list at school were written by white authors. Maybe once in a while, he'd come across a foreign name at the library like Anita Desai or Naguib Mahfouz.

"He's Ismaili, you know," she announced.

"What? No way!" he said, bowled over. He'd never heard of an Ismaili poet or any Ismaili artists, for that matter. Authors, painters, musicians, actors. Nobody. As if they didn't exist. But it made sense. You can't make a living as an artist. So what's the use of it?

"He converted for Pir Shams. Well, that's what some people say. But he's definitely Muslim. They were lovers, maybe, or Pir Shams was just his mentor," she said, scribbling in the margin of the book. "There are different versions of the story."

He was astounded by her openness. No one he knew talked about lovers or gay relationships. He felt he could say anything to her and it would be okay.

"Here." She tucked a bookmark into place then handed him the book. "Borrow it."

"No, that's okay," he said even as he took the book. "I don't know when I'll be able to return it to you."

"How about Thursday at the Beauty Salon?"

"The beauty salon?" Suddenly, he felt conscious of his body the way he did in the locker room at school. He remembered how some of the jocks at school called him a sissy boy. "I'm not into beauty stuff!" he blurted out.

"I bet Prince has manicures and pedicures. I mean, look at him." She pulled her T-shirt taut. "He's hot! But I'm not talking about *that* kind of salon, anyway. This salon is French. The *n* is pronounced nasally." She repeated the word for him, enunciating slowly. "We read poetry, watch films, look at paintings. Anything beautiful," she said with a glint in her eye. "We meet every Thursday at the Forrest Lawn library. Four o'clock sharp."

"Hey, Shaf!" Arzeen called from the bottom of the bleach-ers, waving her arms frantically. "Pappa's here."

Shafina bolted up. "I gotta go."

Ashif stood up, too, his eyes fixed on the image of Prince on her T-shirt. He was in a leather jacket and chains, straddling a Harley. He was also pouting at the camera and his eyes were lined with kohl. She thinks *he's* hot? The thought confounded him, and for the first time, he considered a new idea. Maybe he could be attractive, too.

"Oh, and you'll need one of these for the salon," she said, tapping her beret.

"I've got no plans to be in Paris any time soon."

"Try Kmart," she said with a wink.

He watched as she stepped down the bleachers, the pleats on the back of her skirt swishing like a mermaid's tail.

"How many members do you have?" he called after her.

"Two now," she said, turning back with a smile.

His legs shook with a nervous excitement. He sat down, cradled the book. He'd never met anyone like her. He felt as if he'd been wading in a river all this time when suddenly, he was at its mouth, gushing into the ocean. He flipped open the book. His eyes landed on the line of a poem, underlined in brilliant blue.

You are an ocean in a drop of dew.

Chapter 7

WHEN LAYLA GETS OFF the phone, she's upset. That was Mukhiyani Ma of Headquarters Jamatkhana. She had called to place her regular order, not only for her family, but also for her *phat*, the table of nightly offerings she's responsible for. Today, she asked Layla if she could order her famous chicken samosas, too. Layla refused, but she persisted. "Please, Layla *Bai*, give me the honour. Just this once. Lailatul Qadr is such a big night and I really want something special on my *phat*." She's got such gall! Layla knows she shouldn't be so disrespectful to a jamati leader, but she is annoyed with Mukhiyani Ma. How many times can she say no? If anyone should understand the value of a vow, it should be her. There were countless others who had asked her, too, but most people had the decency to accept her no graciously. Everyone knows that Layla has taken a personal vow to never make her chicken samosas for anyone but the Imam.

She had the privilege of cooking for Khudavind in 1992, his last visit to Canada. "He wants to eat my samosas, again?" she asked the councillor who delivered the good news. She could hardly believe her luck. It was hard enough to believe it the first time. In 1982, Layla won the chicken samosa competition during the Imam's silver jubilee to celebrate the beloved Aga Khan's twenty-five years since he came to the throne of Imamat, which was handed down to him by his grandfather, a direct descendant of the Prophet. The competition was sponsored by the Ismailia Council to ensure that the job, coveted by so many, was given this time to someone on the basis of merit rather than connections. They were in a new world now, and the Imam was keen for them to embrace a new philosophy: meritocracy. "Mediocrity?" she asked Ashif when she first heard the word. "No, Mummy. Meri-toc-racee." He then tried to explain the meaning but she didn't agree with the idea, not that she said anything. She hadn't won the contest on skill alone. She knew there were greater forces at play.

A lacquered portrait of the Imam in a white polo shirt, next to an Arabian horse, hangs on the wall in the living room. A red-and-green rosary is strung around the picture frame like a garland of flowers on a Hindu god, despite the clear but gentle instructions at jamatkhana asking people to please let go of these old traditions. "We are not idol worshippers. We are Ismaili Muslims, not Hindus like our forefathers. And the essence of our faith is esoteric not exoteric." Next to the portrait, mounted in a locked glass display box, is a white plate with a twenty-four-karat-gold fork and knife glued to it like the crossed swords of a royal shield. Underneath, the bronze nameplate reads MRS. LAYLA M. VISRAM, CHICKEN SAMOSA CHAMPION, SILVER JUBILEE 1982.

The Imam had been so impressed by Layla's samosas that he sent her the plate as well as the cutlery he used to eat them. A divine gift! Normally, all items he touched would have been auctioned off to the jamat—like the Mercedes he was driven in, the throne chair he sat on during the ceremonies, or the silver knife he used during a cake-cutting ceremony. Not that any of the items (with the exception of the car) were ever used after they were purchased. That would be sacrilegious. Instead, the items were covered in plastic and placed on display in the homes of the winning bidders. Private museums scattered throughout the city, the country, the world. At first, Layla was hurt when she found out the Imam had not used his bare hands to eat her samosas but then she realized that it was not an insult to her but this is how he ate. After all, he was no ordinary man. He was the Imam! He carried the light of Allah in him. He must eat everything with a fork and knife. Just like the Europeans.

From the kitchen window, Layla sees Mansoor pull into his parking spot. Why is he home so early? It's only six. He doesn't come home until she's back from jamatkhana at nine.

Mansoor walks in with a mess of papers pressed against his chest and his briefcase. "Where's my son?" he asks, setting his things down on the dining table, crushing a napkin shaped into a rose. The table is already set for tomorrow's lunch.

"Tomorrow. He's coming tomorrow for lunch," she says.

"Impossible! He said today."

"No, Tuesday. The day before . . ."

Mansoor doesn't wait for her to finish and walks away. She hears the door of his bedroom open and close. Her bedroom, too. The bathroom.

When he returns, she reminds him that tomorrow is the right date. "The day before Lailatul Qadr, remember?"

"Oh-ho, Layla. How would I know when that is?" He drags a dining chair out and sits down heavily.

She quickly moves a plate setting out of his way.

"Sometimes I can't keep things straight," he says, shaking his head. "Things are slipping away from me . . ."

"Why don't you rest for a little while? Then you'll be fresh."

"There's no time to rest!" he snaps. "I have so much to do. You know that."

"Yes, I know."

"I have to . . . a man cannot go out worse off than how he came in. I have to finish . . ."

"Don't worry, you will finish," she says, though she is not sure what he means.

"You think so?" he asks like a child looking for approval.

"Yes, of course!" she says, trying to cheer him up. "Let me make you some tea, okay?"

"Yes, tea. Let's have tea. That would be nice," he says, slumping back into his chair.

Suddenly, her husband looks so small to her, as if his body has shrunk, and Layla's mind begins to spin with worry.

Layla arrived at Vienna International Airport with a suitcase in one hand and Ashif's hand in the other. He was close to two and now walking and talking. Almost a year after they first arrived in London, she received a letter from Mansoor telling her that he was at an interim camp in Austria. He had sent the letter through a man at his camp who had relatives in London. The man's cousin, Farida, spent months making inquiries before she finally found Layla and Ashif. At first, Farida thought she had found the wrong woman. "But the woman I am looking for only has one child, not two," she said, pointing to the bulge in the blanket tied across Layla's body like a baby sling. "No, no," Layla said, opening the blanket to reveal the hot-water bottle she used to stay warm. "It's me, only. Layla Visram."

At the airport, she spotted Mansoor behind the glass wall of the crowded meeting area with his briefcase between his feet. He was wearing his wedding suit, the one he only wore at their anniversary parties. He had on the metal-tipped shoes, too. It was only when she pulled Ashif closer that she realized how much weight Mansoor had lost. The suit hung on him like a blue gunnysack. Her heart sank, as if into a swamp. What had happened to her husband?

Mansoor raised his arms above his head and frantically waved at them, and her heart lifted. She pulled Ashif by the wrist and ran to him. Mansoor reached first for his son.

"Look at you!" Mansoor kneeled down, his eyes moist with tears. "You're such a big boy!"

"Mummy!" Ashif screamed and locked his arms around his mother's knees.

Mansoor pried his son away from her, despite his kicks and screams, and pressed him tightly to his chest. "Pappa is so happy to see you!" He only returned him to Layla when people in the waiting area shot him dirty looks.

"He just needs some time to get used to things," Layla said, though she needed time, too. She barely recognized him, either.

"You're right," he said and put his arm around her. "Come, let's go."

He then told her he'd made all the arrangements for their new life. They were booked on the first flight to Montreal tomorrow morning. They were moving to Canada. He never asked her how she had coped alone in London, and when she tried to ask him about his final days in Uganda and the camp in Austria, he just shook his head. "What's the use of talking about the past, Layla?"

That night, they stayed at a small inn near the airport. When they made love, she could feel the bones of his rib cage.

Chapter 8

FROM HER KITCHEN WINDOW, Layla watches children scatter as a limousine winds its way through the inner road of the townhouse complex. Pedestrians stop, trying to make out who's behind the tinted windows. "He's here!" she shouts. She peels off her apron and tosses it on the kitchen counter. Underneath, an A-shaped dress patterned with tiny roses that she bought this morning. A new lipstick, too.

At his desk in the living room, Mansoor stands up to face the window. A driver with a chauffeur's hat jumps out of a limousine and rushes to pull open the back door. An arm holding a briefcase extends, but then the prairie sun escapes from behind a cloud and turns the window into a mirror. Now all Mansoor can see is an image of himself.

Ashif walks up the front steps with a massive heart-shaped balloon attached to a bouquet of red roses. Inside, he's hidden his mother's spa certificate. He doesn't want his father to know.

At the front door, Layla taps her hair to make sure it's in place and checks her lipstick.

"Aye, Layla, he's not a guest. This is the boy's home." Mansoor throws open the front door. Sunshine pours into the house. Tucked under his arm, two copies of his business plan, and a new set of loan forms he drew up with Ashif as a silent partner.

Layla starts crying the minute she sees him.

Ashif sets his briefcase down and takes her in his arms. "Hi, Mummy."

"You're going to ruin your makeup," Mansoor says.

Ashif gently pushes her back. "But she still looks beautiful." He gives her the roses.

"Why, son? You shouldn't waste your money," she says, wiping her tears.

"She's right. They'll be dead within days," Mansoor says, feeling slighted. Not only did he say hello to his mother first, but his son did not bring him a gift. He never does.

Ashif reaches a hand out to his father. "Hi, Pappa."

"Good to see you, son!" Mansoor shakes his son's hand heartily. "Come in. Come in. Let's go to my office, catch up before lunch."

"But the food!" Layla protests. "It will get cold."

"You can rewarm it, Layla. I have things to talk to my son about." Mansoor reaches for his son's arm.

"Let's eat first, Pappa. I'm really hungry," Ashif says, though he'd had breakfast on his flight.

Layla is elated. She hooks her arm in her son's and leads him inside.

Mansoor feels a flicker of anger. His son needs to show him

more respect! But he doesn't say anything. He's bigger than that. "Yes, yes. Let's eat," he says and follows them in.

"So, what is your meeting about, son?" Mansoor asks, his elbows planted on the dining table as he mixes a plateful of chicken biryani with the fingers of one hand.

"The company's restructuring," Ashif says, dipping a piece of *dhokra* into the date-tamarind chutney.

"Downsizing?" Mansoor leans over his plate and stuffs a fistful of rice into his mouth.

"Yup." Ashif glances at the TV in the living room, which is turned to the news, but set to mute. The image behind the anchorman shows a sheep with a nameplate that reads DOLLY around its neck. The headline above reads WILL THERE EVER BE ANOTHER YOU?

"Part of the sales force is being automated," he adds.

"It's a brave new world, son! The digital revolution." He taps the copy of his business plan that's tucked under his thigh, readying himself to share his news.

"They're laying off about twenty percent globally. Over the next six months."

Mansoor raises his eyebrows. "Got to run a tight ship. Get rid of slackers."

Layla puts one *rotli* on Mansoor's plate, then the other on Ashif's, before adding the rest to a stack in the middle of the table.

"Efficiency is the name of the game." Mansoor picks up the piece of chicken and pops it into his mouth. "And it's technology that will lead the way."

"Come on, sit with us," Ashif implores Layla. He wants his mother to relax and join them instead of running around catering to them like she's their waitress. He also doesn't want to be alone with his father, especially now that the subject has switched from the weather and the news to business. Like a preacher at his pulpit, it's always a one-way conversation.

"I'm coming, *bheta*," Layla says. "You eat, eat."

"Yes, eat, son. Don't worry about your mother." Mansoor folds his *rotli* and rips it into two.

"Come soon, Mummy," Ashif says. He knows she's fasting, but he wants her to join them anyway, instead of serving them like she's the hired help.

"Take more, *bheta*." Layla holds a spoonful of biryani over Ashif's plate.

"No, Mummy." Ashif bars his plate with his hands. "I already have so much."

"Eh-hey, don't force him," Mansoor says to her. "He's not a child."

"Okay. A little more." Ashif lays his hand back on his lap. He's told her so many times that he doesn't eat fried foods. She should bake the cassava or substitute olive oil for the ghee. It's much healthier. But he doesn't want to make a fuss and he knows it will only offend her.

Layla piles a scoopful of chicken biryani onto his plate.

"Eat, *bheta*. Before it gets cold," she says joyfully. She throws another potato-*champ* and three more pieces of cassava onto his plate.

"Everything's delicious, Mummy." Ashif rakes his fork over the rice. "As usual."

The bouquet of roses sits on the deep freezer. The heart-shaped balloon sways from side to side like a hand waving to get someone's attention.

"Then I am happy." She pulls her son's head to her with the base of her palm and kisses him.

Her hands feel rough against Ashif's skin. Her skin is dry and cracked, her fingernails chewed to the base. He's even more pleased about the spa certificate he'd chosen for her. She'll be able to relax and enjoy herself, for a day, at least. "Me, too, Mummy. I'm happy."

Layla kisses him again. Watching Ashif eat gives her a deep sense of satisfaction.

Mansoor taps the jug of empty water. "Can you bring ice?" He removes a neatly folded embossed handkerchief from his pants pocket and dabs his forehead and chin.

Layla picks up the jug and disappears back into the kitchen.

"Do you need a backup plan at the company?" Mansoor asks. "Just in case?"

"No, of course not," Ashif says, irritated by the question. "My job is safe."

"Never a good idea to be so confident." Mansoor taps his hand on his plate, but several grains of rice stick stubbornly to his fingers. "You always need a plan B." Mansoor notices his son's clothing. Is he or isn't he going to an important business meeting? No tie, no jacket? A pair of sunglasses on his head? Sure, Mansoor knows about casual Fridays. A perk of the job, one of his customers explained. But it wasn't Friday today. Besides, what kind of perk is that, anyway? Don't they know slack dress can only lead to slack work habits? And then how do you tell the difference between a businessman and those who work in the lower classes? His son looks like he is on vacation. What kind of impression is he going to make with his superiors?

"I'm on solid ground, trust me," Ashif says.

"You never know when the wolf will be at your door." Mansoor snaps the tip off a green chili with his front teeth. "What will you do when they lay you off?"

Ashif laughs. Lay him off? He wishes. Yet he's also offended by his father's assumption. In one quick rush, like a tightly shut valve suddenly opened, he tells his father about the executive track and all the perks that come with it: the salary, the benefits, the stock options. He tells him about Rick's words of confidence, too: One day, he might be running the company. He feels an immediate sense of relief and regret.

Mansoor looks up from his plate, his eyebrows raised. "Executive track?"

Ashif watches his father's surprise turn to pride, and for a moment, he feels the warmth of his gaze spreading through him.

"Why didn't you say anything earlier? By God, that's great news!" Mansoor slaps the table with both hands. He pushes his chair back and shoots up to standing. "Well done, my boy! I always knew you were destined for great things. We've got the next Steve Jobs sitting here!"

"I'm not on the executive track. Not yet. . . ." Why did he say it? His father is now like a runaway train. He has the urge to jump in front and force it to a screeching halt. Or just lie down on the tracks. Ashif knows better. Why can't he control himself?

"Layla!" Mansoor calls, grabbing a bottle of Johnny Walker from the lower cabinet of the dining hutch. The bottle is tucked behind a stack of platters and casserole dishes. Layla insists that he keep his spirits out of sight. She does not want to offend her friends or her customers, all of whom are Ismaili. "Bring ice." He pinches two tumblers out of the upper cabinet. "Layla! Are you listening?" He returns to his chair holding the bottle of whisky by the neck. "An executive, *huh*? Excellent news, son, most excellent."

Layla returns to the dining room with the jug of ice water.

"Not for the water." Mansoor twists open the bronze cap.

Layla frowns. "Oh-ho, *that* at this hour?" She puts the jug down on the table.

"I don't want any," Ashif says, though he would love a drink right now. But he wants to respect his mother's wishes.

Layla fishes ice cubes out of the jug of water and dumps them into a bowl with a fork.

"Don't be shy, son." Mansoor pours several fingers of whisky in each glass. He is thrilled that the boy is pretending he doesn't want any. It is just his way of showing his father some respect. It is not normal, after all, for a child to drink with his parents. A toast first and then he will whisk his son away to his office and show him his business-plan presentation. Make him sign the loan papers. Mansoor grabs a few ice cubes from the bowl and plunges them into the whisky. "Come on, son. We need to celebrate."

"What is the good news?" Layla asks.

"Our son is on his way up," Mansoor says, his eyes lit up, his voice quivering slightly. All his years of fathering had not been wasted. His boy was going to be somebody! "He's getting a promotion."

Layla claps her hands. "Of course he is." Layla wraps her hands around Ashif's face and kisses him on both cheeks. "*Mumbarki, bheta.*"

Ashif turns his fork upside down on his plate. "It's not a promotion, Mummy. Not yet. Maybe in the future."

"You mean you don't have it on paper?" Mansoor hesitates as he hands Ashif a glass. "You should always get things on paper."

Ashif takes the whisky and sets it on the table at a distance in front of him. "It's not a sure thing, Pappa. That's what I am trying to tell you."

Mansoor extends his glass to Ashif in a toast. "He's being too modest. Bottoms up, executive sir."

Ashif raises his glass slowly. When they clink, another valve opens, and before he knows it, he's telling his father he doesn't want to be on the executive track. He's not cut out for this job.

Mansoor laughs. "That makes no sense. Who doesn't want a promotion?" Is his son lying? Maybe there's no promotion at all. He's getting laid off but he's too embarrassed to say. He doesn't know whether to finish his whisky or not.

"There are just a lot of qualified people who want to get on that track," Ashif says in an effort to turn the conversation.

Mansoor wags a finger at Ashif playfully. "Don't tell me you are afraid of a little competition? Come on, have some confidence, will you?" He double punches the air. "You can knock your opponent to the ground." He looks at Layla. "What do you think, Layla? Who's going to win? Our son or some fool idiot?"

"Our son, who else?" Layla says proudly. She pulls out a chair and sits down next to her husband.

"See, son! Your mother and I have the utmost confidence in you. We are here by your side."

"But it's not a done deal, Pappa," Ashif says, trying to gnaw his way out of this trap.

"Come, son. Let's make a list." Mansoor pulls out the pen angled between the buttons of his shirt. "Let's be clear-headed about this. We'll mark down your competitors' strengths and weaknesses. Mark down yours, too. Then figure out a way to beat them."

"Look, Pappa. I'll try my best," Ashif says to appease him. "It's not as if I don't have a good job already." He checks his wristwatch under the table then takes a gulp of whisky.

"Oh-ho, who said you don't have a good job?" Mansoor says, half-laughing.

"Yes, such a good job. Top-notch, isn't it?" Layla adds.

"Aye, Layla. No one asked you." Mansoor clucks his tongue. "We are talking business here. Can't I speak to my son in peace for once?"

Ashif leans forward in his seat, his hands clenched into fists on his lap. He is about to tell his father not to speak to his mother like that when Layla widens her eyes and shakes her head ever so slightly at him, as if to say, Don't make it worse, son. We'll talk when we are alone. Ashif sits back in his chair and reaches for his whisky again.

Mansoor takes another sip, too. "Look, son, I know you have a good job. No one is saying otherwise. But how difficult is it to make it to middle management? Don't be so easily satisfied, son. Every Tom, Dick, and Raja is working at these big corporations nowadays. Good for them. Good for you. But there's a reason they call it middle management. It's far from the top. Believe you me, son, the consequence of mediocrity is death."

"But I'm happy with my job." Ashif feels as though he's pushing against a boulder, one that will soon give way and flatten him.

Mansoor swirls his empty glass absently. His son has so

much potential and the gumption, yet his drive seems to wax and wane like a penny stock. He's seen this behaviour before. Just when Ashif is winning a race, he wants to slow down and rest. Makes no sense. He needs to push him harder.

"Do you know that the average CEO makes one hundred and four times—that's right, one hundred and four times— more than the average worker? Read that in *Fortune 500*. The benefits of being on top are endless. First and foremost: everyone knows your name. That's when you have real power."

"I make enough money." Ashif drops his arm under the table to steal another glance at his watch. Don't say anything more and prolong the torture. I'll be out of here soon.

Mansoor keeps a smile on his face but the vein in his forehead is throbbing. Look at the smug look on Ashif's face. Bragging to *him* about *his* salary. Who does he think he is? If Mansoor had said such a thing, his father would have given him a thrashing. When his father entered the room, the children stood up in unison, as if they were greeting an army officer, welcoming a king. They never made direct eye contact with him, not only when they were young, but well into adulthood, even after they were married and had their own children. They were still his children. It was his right to demand their respect and they gave it to him unconditionally. No talking back. No disagreeing with him. No questioning him. It was a form of insolence and met with force. Meanwhile, Mansoor has never even laid a hand on Ashif. Even when he deserved it! He decided long ago to veer away from his father's brand of parenting. He wanted to be a modern father. He would never strong-arm his son. Instead, he would discuss things with him. Rationally and coolly. But who would stand for *this* level of disrespect? Still it won't do to lose his temper. He breathes in deeply and calms himself. He needs to win his boy over.

"Look, son, all I am saying is, why settle? Take the example of world-class athletes. You think Gretzky got to the top by sitting on his laurels? How about Tiger Woods? Even the women these days are making the A-lists. Look at Serena and Venus Williams. Just put your mind to it, and before you know it, you too will be rocketing to the top. Business is in our blood."

"Yes, Pappa. You're right, Pappa," Ashif says. He's knocked out. As if he'd been in a boxing match. There's only one way to deal with his father: keep your mouth shut.

"Excellent, son," Mansoor says. He knew a sports analogy would work. A knockout punch! Sports and business are, after all, the universal language of men. "That's all I wanted to hear, son. Just give it your all. You can do it." Mansoor wants to add that if it wasn't for the sheer determination and drive of those young athletes' fathers, it's doubtful they would have amounted to anything. Look at Walter Gretzky, Earl Woods, Richard Williams. They were the ones who set the course for their children, pushed them to their maximum potential.

He's gearing up for round two when the limousine driver taps on his horn, just as Ashif had asked him.

"I have to go," Ashif says, standing up from the table.

"Already?" Layla asks.

Mansoor stands, too. "But I still have some items to discuss with you, son." He picks up his business plan and loan papers from his seat.

"You haven't even seen Shamma and Almas Masi, either," Layla says.

"Sorry, my meetings start soon," Ashif says, slipping on his jacket. "I can't be late."

"Of course! Go, son. He doesn't have time to waste on those old ladies, Layla. Isn't that right, son? You have big business to tend to."

Layla follows Ashif to the front door with a bulging plastic bag. As he puts his shoes on, she pulls a wrinkled set of forms out from the bag and hands them to him. "I found these behind your father's desk when I was cleaning."

"What is it?" he asks, examining the papers, but it doesn't take long for him to figure it out. Commercial bank loan forms with his father's name, the house as collateral, and a large sum of money written under "Funds Requested." He scrunches up the forms and pitches them at the wall, clipping the mirror. It swings dangerously. "Not again!" he says, clenching his jaw.

"Please, *bheta*. Keep your voice down." She nervously looks over her shoulder. "Your father will hear." She scoops up the forms and stuffs them into her apron pocket.

"He's in debt again?" he asks in a harsh whisper. "Unbelievable!"

She shrugs. "You know him. He doesn't tell anyone anything. Least of all me. But what else can it be?"

Ashif pounds his fist into the palm of his other hand. He wants to march into his father's office and straighten that man out. Once and for all. But he knows he can't. He needs to control himself for his mother's sake. An argument with him will only make things hard for her after he leaves, and that's the last thing he wants.

"Now I understand why he's been working so hard," she says. "I wake up to go to morning prayers, and there he is, at his desk in a suit, working already. Sometimes he is even talking to himself. I come home from jamatkhana in the evening, same story. Working, working, working. All the time. And at his age? No wonder his mind is *kachumber*. All jumbled up these days. And if I tell him he needs to rest, take it easy, he only eats my head. I don't know what to do, *bheta*. The business is going to be the death of him." Her voice is trembling, her eyes moist.

The ground beneath Ashif turns to quicksand. The same sinking feeling. He feels he can't breathe. He takes his mother into his arms. "Please, Mummy. Don't cry."

"We need to help him, son. Please. Once he solves his business problems, he will be okay."

He knows by *we* she means *you* and he also knows what he needs to do. His stomach clenches into knots. "Don't worry, Mummy. I'm going to take care of everything."

She reaches up and kisses him. "Thank you, *bheta*."

At his desk, Mansoor can hear Ashif and Layla though he can't make out their words. They're at it again! He slaps his pen to the table. Whispering to each other like schoolgirls. Even when Ashif was a teenager, if Mansoor happened to walk in on them chatting, they would stop, change the topic. Was this any way to treat a father? Why is Layla gossiping with him, anyway? Telling him her secrets, maybe even complaining about him? A boy does not want to know about these things— things meant for a woman. A daughter, not a son. Is it any wonder his son has turned out so soft? A sissy boy who can't even keep his job. That's his mother's fault! He should never have trusted her to take care of him on her own. But what choice did he have? He had to move to Rocky Mountain House. He only did what countless men before him did. His father, too. Not to mention war heroes. Men who leave their families temporarily because they have to. After all, taking care of business is taking care of family and that is every man's greatest honour and responsibility.

Mansoor pushes his chair back from his desk. "What's going on in there?" he calls out.

There's a moment of silence then Layla answers. "Nothing, nothing. Just saying goodbye."

"Let him go, will you, Layla? You're going to make him late for work."

"I'm going, Pappa," Ashif interjects. He balls his hands into fists and jams them into his pockets. "Just saying goodbye."

"Okay," Mansoor replies, still irritated. Ten hours just to say goodbye? No matter how much he's done for his son, he only has eyes for his mother. He is her *chumcho*! Ever ready to do anything she wants. Meanwhile, he constantly pushes back against his father, as he did at lunch. What has he done to deserve his son's contempt? It's a question that plagues him daily, like a mosquito buzzing at his ear that he can't swat away. He can't think of a thing. On the contrary, he has fulfilled his every duty to his son, no matter what the circumstance, and this—*this*—is how he chooses to treat him? His face flushes hot with anger. He grabs the loan forms and tears them to pieces. He'll find another way to secure the money.

"Don't forget this, *bheta*," Layla says, handing Ashif the plastic bag filled with containers of food, plastic cutlery, and serviettes. "In case you get hungry at the hotel."

He's about to explain that he can order room service, but a wave of exhaustion spreads through him. It won't make a difference. He takes the bag from her and thanks her.

His father arrives just as he is about to leave. "Better go, son. Otherwise you will give your superiors a bad impression."

"Come back soon," Layla says and starts crying. "Or tomorrow for Lailatul Qadr."

"Or better yet, why don't you come back for the weekend after your meetings in Vancouver?" Mansoor asks.

"Yes! Please come back." Layla gives him another hug.

"It will make us very happy, son," Mansoor adds. "I can pay for any change fees for your flight, too."

"I can't, Pappa. I'm sorry," he says, irritated by the offer. As usual, his father has no concept of money. He extends his hand to his father, relieved to finally be at the end of his visit.

"Very well, Mr. Executive Sir," Mansoor says, grasping the limp-fish fingers of his son's hand. Was it always this weak? A strong handshake—*that's* a man's business card. A man's power is in his body, everyone knows that.

Chapter 9

IN THE BACK OF the limousine, Ashif struggles to breathe. His father's loan is going to wipe out his savings. He'll have to start again. Stay at his job longer. At least another decade. He gasps for air. He tries to open his window. It's locked. He bangs on the glass separating him from the driver. The partition rolls down. He yells at the driver to stop. The driver pulls onto the shoulder, screeches to a halt. Ashif throws open the door. Stumbles down the embankment into a field of snow. He sucks in the cold air. In and out. He can't get enough. In and out. He's desperate. As if he's dying.

When Ashif was a child, he didn't like crowds or too much noise. Not even excessive light. He found it overwhelming. And exhausting. Like an overloaded machine that shuts down. Instead, he preferred to stay in his room and read fairy tales or make up little stories. He could do it for hours on end, without ever getting bored, as if he was lost in a wonderous world that he never wanted to leave.

One day his father found his notebooks. The boxfuls of stories he kept under his bed. Ashif was sure he'd love them. But he didn't. He wasn't mad, he told him, but disappointed that he was wasting his time. He was old enough to know better. He was now eight. Ashif tried to explain. These were his science journals. His observations. That's what his teacher, Ms. Clarke, called them. But his father said she was wrong. This was not science. It was fiction and it had no value.

"It'll only distract you from important subjects like math and science. The ones that really count." His father then told him he had no choice but to take his notebooks away.

"Please, Pappa. Don't," he begged, his voice cracking.

"No crying, okay?"

"But I love them, Pappa. . . ." Ashif said, unable to stop his tears.

"This is not the kind of thing to love!" His voice was firm and strong.

A new thought pelted him like a hailstone. There must be something wrong with him. Why else did he love something he wasn't supposed to? He was ashamed of himself.

"Trust me, son," his father said as he pulled out the other boxes from under his bed. "One day, you'll thank me."

Ashif stood at his bedroom window, frozen in place. In the street below, his father piled the boxes into his Chevy. His father never told him what he did with his notebooks and he never asked. That night, he wet his bed. When his mother found the soiled sheets crumpled under his bed, he begged her not to tell his father. She didn't. On that day or the many times after. He couldn't bear the idea of his father finding out there was yet something else wrong with him. Then his father would stop loving him for sure.

"Sir! Are you alright?" the driver calls out to him from the road.

Ashif comes back. "Yes, fine. Just a bout of asthma."

Back inside the limousine, Ashif calls his broker and arranges to cash out his investments. Then he calls his mother. He asks her to tell his father to meet him for breakfast in the Air Canada business lounge tomorrow. He doesn't want his father to come to his hotel, even if it's right there. When she asks if everything is okay, he says he's taking care of everything, just as he promised. "Don't worry. Pappa's going to be fine. We all are."

"Thank you, *bheta*," she says. "You are the best son."

At the airport, the limousine pulls into the U-shaped driveway of his hotel. The driver jumps out and holds the door open for him. Ashif steps out with his briefcase. A doorman wearing a red uniform adorned with gold buttons opens the hotel doors.

"Welcome, sir," he says.

Ashif hands him the bag of food from his mother. "Can you throw this out for me, please?"

"Of course, sir."

Ashif straightens his suit jacket, then marches into the lobby full of businessmen.

Chapter 10

WHEN LAYLA TELLS MANSOOR that Ashif wants to meet him for breakfast, he's confused. His son never wants to see him without his mother. Then it becomes clear: his son's loyalties are shifting back to him. What else could it be? He asked Ashif to come back and now he has. Mansoor has waited for such a long time for this moment. He laughs. He has been right all along. That's all his son needed. The proper guidance to do the right thing. That's all every child needs.

When Ashif was a child, he noticed the boy's oddities. He spent much of his time alone instead of playing with other children. He was always so quiet, too, as if he was lost inside himself. He could lie on the grass and stare at the clouds for hours. He'd even seen him with his ear pressed against a tree, as if listening for a heartbeat. This wasn't normal behaviour! He worried his son would be bullied at school—odd children always are, especially boys.

He didn't want Ashif to stick out. Like so many who came to this country. People who preferred their old ways, glued together like a herd of sheep. Wasn't that the reason Amin threw them out to begin with? Mansoor was clear. He would not repeat the mistakes of Uganda. You have to get along with the people you live amongst. Assimilate! He would never return to Uganda, either, like those who galloped back the second Indians were invited back. Fine. Go. Who wants people like them, anyway? As if Canada was just a stopover. Not for Mansoor. He was committed to this country and this country alone. It was the only way to have deep roots and build a real home. There was nothing he wanted more for his family. His son would have to learn how to stand out for the right reasons (talent and accomplishment) but blend in otherwise. It was a crucial for his success here.

Mansoor had always assumed Ashif would outgrow his odd behaviour, but when he hadn't by age eight, he knew he would have to take things into his own hands. He decided to cut the problem out at its root. Like amputating an extra pinky finger. The hand might feel strange for a little while, but in good time, the body forgets. It always does. Just like the time he found all those boxes of Ashif's diaries. He didn't beat him like his father would have. Instead, he calmly explained why writing and reading fiction were an utter waste of time. His son was upset at first, but in due course, he complied with the right behaviour.

Mansoor naturally helped matters along by removing all bad influences from his son's life. First and foremost, his teacher, Ms. Clarke. What kind of teacher can't differentiate between facts and fiction? He removed him from that school immediately and enrolled him in one with a solid track record in winning math and science awards. He also encouraged him to join the debate club and sports teams. He taught him about how to joke with people, put him in elocution classes. He also rewarded every success. An ice cream for a goal, a nickel for the right answer. Pavlov knew what he was doing. Eventually, Ashif came to him with his own ideas. Attending a hockey game together, joining Toastmasters. He excelled at his new pursuits and brought home top marks. Trophies, too! He shudders to think what would have happened if he hadn't intervened. Thankfully he did. His son is who he is today because of him.

Yet Ashif is off track again. It was only a matter of time until he was laid off, maybe even fired. He'd always assumed that his company, with its deep pockets, would have trained him properly. It was the only reason he let him stay in Toronto after business school. He had expected him to come back home, armed with a strong set of business skills and a solid Rolodex, to take over the family business. Yet all his company has managed to do is to give him a big head. He seems to think he's better than everyone else—his father included. As if. Mansoor could do his job with his eyes closed, and for half the money to boot.

Mansoor would have to take things into his own hands if he wanted to fix his son again. The solution was clear. He'd take Ashif under his wing at the business. Train him from the ground up. M.G. Visram & Sons Dry Cleaners, *Unlimited*. That's what he had once envisioned. A big family, working together like a well-oiled machine. They'd keep their resources—talent, labour, money—within the family. That's how empires are built. He had wanted more children—boys or girls, it didn't matter. Women were capable of anything these days. Look at Margaret Thatcher, Oprah Winfrey, Benazir Bhutto. They didn't stop until they reached the top. Good for them. Instead, they hired other women to help them with their duties at home. Cooking, cleaning, taking care of children—low-paying positions that could easily be covered by their high-powered salaries. It made complete sense. A division of labour. Exactly how Ford revolutionized the automobile industry. Now that was progress! He would have gladly welcomed a daughter into the business. Let her stand shoulder-to-shoulder with him. But he never had the chance. There were no daughters, no other sons. Only Ashif, and he would have to do.

If only he had taken Ashif under his wing sooner. Maybe it would have been easier. Children are more pliable. His own apprenticeship started at the age of four, when he was required to accompany his father to the store each morning before school, where his father sat him on the counter next to the cash register. He was not allowed to ask any questions or make any requests, and at the end of each visit, he was quizzed to test his understanding. Short, clear answers in English—the language he was required to master before mastering five others. Any wrong answers, any misbehaviour, was punished immediately.

His father's laugh booms behind him. "Fool idiot! It's too late. Your son is almost thirty. Thirty! And you are sixty."

"No, Pappa!" he says defiantly. "I'm going to do it. Train my son. Get the money for my plant. You just watch me!"

His father jams his cane into his back. "Don't be smart with me!"

Mansoor folds over in pain.

"You better do it, boy! Everything depends on it."

Tick-tock, tick-tock, tick-tock.

Chapter 11

ASHIF AND MEL, THE VP of human resources, meet briefly before the first layoff candidate arrives in a conference room at the hotel. Their protocol was simple. Ashif would lead at the start. His job was to make the candidate feel comfortable. Then Mel would take over.

Most of the candidates are surprised by the news, some devastated, a few are thrilled. Ashif tries his best to be present, to be empathetic. Most of them have a family, children, mortgages. Most of them are over forty. But as the candidates discuss their futures, Ashif's mind returns to a time he thought he'd have a very different life.

He met Shafina each Thursday in the same room at the Forrest Lawn Library from four to six p.m. for their Beauty Salons. The room had a wooden table, four rickety chairs, a TV-VCR, and a boom box with a double cassette player. Each week they devoured poetry, plays, films, novels, music, art catalogues. From *Flashdance* to *That Obscure Object of Desire*, Annie Lennox to Bach, Shakespeare to Lorca. Everything at the library and anything they could get their hands on with the help of the librarian, Mrs. Sims, who could access libraries across the city and the country, too.

Some of the books they wanted to read posed a problem. *Lolita, Delta of Venus, Giovanni's Room, Shame, The Unicorn and the Dancing Girl, Wifey,* Rumi's *The Book of Love: Poems on Ecstasy and Longing.* They couldn't take them home without eliciting parental scrutiny. From her parents, anyway. His mother assumed any book he was reading was a school book. She also left him to handle anything to do with school. She didn't know the Canadian system, but she trusted it implicitly. She rarely checked to see if he'd finished his homework, never asked which classes he liked, or what his teachers were like. He didn't mind. In fact, he liked it. He could do whatever he wanted. He even signed his own parental permission forms, even his absentee notes when he and Shafina skipped school. His mother knew he could forge her signature, but she had agreed only so he could deposit the cheques his father left them on his Sunday visits.

They decided to cover their books—controversial or not— just in case. It became a Beauty Salon ritual. They only used paper from a Japanese shop on Stephen Avenue, cutting it to fit the book jacket. They'd stencil the same two letters on the spine with their calligraphy set. *B.S.*

"That's what you call a perfect cover," Ashif said, holding up their first book.

"Maybe we should use B.B. instead? Burqa Books," she said, and they laughed even though Ismaili women didn't wear burqas. They'd read about a concept called *taqiyya*, which Ismailis used to practise along with other Muslim communities who were persecuted for their differing interpretations of Islam. They would dissimulate, pretend to be anything but Ismaili in an effort to protect themselves. "But that's a kind of burqa, isn't it? Because you have to hide who you really are," she said and he agreed. She was so smart.

Into each book jacket they tucked their favourite poem, "Speak" by Faiz Ahmed Faiz. A poetic "fuck you" to potential censors, especially their parents.

At one salon, without warning, Shafina threw her arms around his neck and kissed him. He kept his eyes open, his heart thumping with terror and excitement.

"Is it your first time?" she asked when they came up for air.

"Yeah," Ashif said, embarrassed.

"You're a natural," she said and pulled him back in.

After that day, their Beauty Salons turned into make-out salons. That's all they wanted to do. Kiss and touch each other. They hid themselves in the library stairwell or behind the study room door until eventually they found a solution. They papered the glass wall and on it, they drew a few lines and some dots, a guise for an art project.

"What's this?" Mrs. Sims asked, pointing to the wall when she walked in on them without knocking.

They scrambled to sit up, pulling down their T-shirts.

"It's against library rules," Mrs. Sims said. "You need to take it down."

"But we're mapping the world," Shafina said. "See those lines . . ."

"Yes," she said.

"They're outlines of the continents. And those dots—they're all the cities we want to visit."

"Doesn't look much like a map to me," she said.

Ashif piped in. "That's because it's impressionistic. You know, like Van Gogh. A map of the world like a constellation of stars."

Mrs. Sims examined the wall again. "Oh, yes! How very lovely. Good work, you two."

When she left, they burst out laughing. "We're a good team," she said and he pulled her in for another make-out session.

Each evening and on weekends, they spoke on the phone for endless hours. Sometimes they were on the phone all night, falling in and out of sleep between their conversations. Other times, they'd say nothing, just listen to each other breathe. That's when he knew he loved her. He felt with her what he'd never felt with anyone else. That he was at home. He could relax and be himself. When he finally found the courage to tell her, she said she loved him, too. "Forever and ever, *chéri.*"

Now, all they wanted was to make love. But where? He wasn't allowed at her house—her father was too strict. She was welcome at his house, but his mother was always home and expected them to sit and have tea with her. She was ecstatic that he had an Ismaili girlfriend and even happier to have her company. "It's just so nice to have a girl around," she told Shafina. They tried to escape to his room, but his mother insisted they keep the door open.

His father was moving back from Rocky Mountain House soon. Ashif missed him even if he was used to his absence. It had been four years since he left. But there were other reasons he was looking forward to having him back home. Without him, Ashif had to run errands for his mom, take her grocery shopping, do the family banking, accompany her to community events, or just keep her company. Finally, he'd be able to shuck these duties and be a normal teenager. Best of all, he'd finally have more time alone with Shafina.

They started researching universities away from home. Columbia, the Sorbonne, the American University in Cairo, and McGill were at the top of their lists. They sent away for course calendars and eagerly checked the mail for their arrival. When the packages arrived, they spent hours mocking up class schedules for their first year, like mapping out a travel itinerary. "The scenic route," she joked. Art history, film and photography, architecture, urban planning, linguistics, French, Arabic, international politics, the modern novel, natural science, macroeconomics.

Neither one of them was sure what they wanted to do yet, but she was leaning toward something in the visual arts, maybe film or photography. He was leaning toward the letters, maybe journalism or else poetry. "That makes sense, *chéri*. You have a poetic heart," she said and he was elated. That day, he bought a stack of notebooks and started writing again. As if he was resurrecting a part of himself. He papered his notebooks like their B.S. books. He didn't want his father to ever find out.

"What if we don't get accepted to the same university?" he asked when the terrible thought first occurred to him. He could no longer imagine life without her.

"No one can separate our hearts, *mon chéri*," she said. "We'll always be under the same sky. Just like Rumi and Shams."

After their meetings, Mel and Ashif debrief and have a quick dinner together. He likes her and he senses she likes him, too. But he knows he'll never confide in her. They need to maintain a professional distance. So many rules, so many lines, like wands of light in a security system. You can't cross one without an alarm being set off and showing up as a black mark on your next performance review. Merit is important, but how well you get along with people is just as important if you want to move up at the company. You have to attend endless client dinners and events. You have to participate in employee activities outside of work hours—golf tournaments, the company baseball team, weekly drinks at the local bar or during high season, every weeknight. You have to speak about sports, and, in the company of only men, women's bodies. You have to follow the rules. He finds it exhausting. But he does it anyway. He has to if he wants to fit in. He's always wearing a mask. A constant impostor. Not just at work, but in every part of his life. So that no one knows him. He has no one to confide in. Not Caity, not his friends from business school that he meets with once or twice a year. He doesn't feel at home anywhere. He feels untethered, even to his own body. As if he might float away at any second.

Chapter 12

MANSOOR ARRIVES AT THE Air Canada business lounge dressed in his best business suit: a charcoal three-piece with a freshly laundered white shirt; a blue pinstriped tie, tied into a fat Windsor knot. He carries a briefcase and, in his jacket pocket, a silver-embossed card holder with his son's initials.

The plush lounge is packed with men in smart suits, conducting business meetings. Striking deals. Exactly the kind of place he and his son should be. He straightens, feeling taller and more muscular, as if he's taking up more space, as he strides to the host.

"Good morning!" Mansoor says enthusiastically.

The host looks up from his desk and smiles. "Good morning, sir. Are you a member?"

"No. But my son is," Mansoor announces loudly. "Mr. Ashif M. Visram. Elite member."

The host punches some keys on his computer keyboard. "Yes, of course."

"That's my son, you see. Maybe you know him?"

"Could be."

Imagine, they know his son here.

The host steps out from behind his podium. "Please follow me, sir."

Mansoor walks behind him. The work stations and tables are full of white men. A few wear Stetsons with their suits, like financial cowboys. Maybe he should have worn his Stetson, too. No, he looks much more distinguished than any one of them. Of course he does. He's probably done more business than most of them will ever do. He stumbles on the thick carpet. A few tables turn to look.

The host leads him to a window table and pulls a chair out for him. Outside, morning light bathes the tarmac, and in the distance, the fields extend to the horizon and merge with the endless prairie sky. The host snaps open a napkin. Mansoor takes it from him before he can lay it on his lap. The host hands him a menu and lays another on the second setting across from him. "A waiter will be right with you, sir."

Mansoor nods. He unlocks his briefcase and retrieves all its contents: two pens, two calculators, two copies of his business plan, a short list of properties, the silver-plated business-card holder. He arranges them on the chair next to him, setting the card holder on top. He reviews the agenda, which he typed up last night. Reading the words, so carefully arranged on the page, slows the chaotic beating of his heart.

Eight o'clock sharp and there's Ashif walking across the room. He looks so smart with his navy-coloured suit and expensive briefcase. He watches as his son stops and says hello to a few men. My son knows *these* men? He feels a giddy excitement run through him. He waves. Ashif smiles, waggling two fingers in the air. "Two minutes," he mouths. Mansoor nods, gives his son a thumbs-up.

A new thought occurs to him—maybe Ashif knows someone at City Hall. Maybe he even knows the mayor? Imagine. If not personally, then surely one of his contacts will know him. Who knew his son was on friendly terms with such top-class men? Men who push open doors with the snap of a finger. Open sesame. They get anything they want. Just like him in Uganda.

Mansoor glances again at Ashif. He's now chatting with two men at another table. Yes, his son will surely be able to help him—help their company—cut through the red tape and secure the necessary meetings at the City. There's nothing they can't do together. He and his son!

"Sorry I'm late." Ashif takes a deep breath as he sets his briefcase down.

Mansoor stands to greet his son. "No problem, son. You are worth waiting for. Terrific choice, this place," he says.

"I'm glad you like it," Ashif says and they both sit down.

"Coffee, sir?" the waiter asks, holding a carafe over Ashif's cup.

"Yes," Ashif replies.

"Are you ready to order?"

"Have you looked at the menu, Pappa?"

Mansoor slips on his bifocals and reviews the menu. It is printed on thick stock and does not have many choices. He runs his finger down the list of items. Some of the items are strange and exotic: bison breakfast burger, potatoes in bécha-mel sauce, lobster frittata, truffled scrambled eggs. What are these things? He does not want to ask the waiter and he will definitely not ask Ashif. What will his son think—that his father knows nothing? Instead, he searches for something familiar. Thirty-eighty dollars for steak and eggs? Is it made with gold or what? Forget the price, he decides. This is a cele-bration and money is of no importance. Maybe later they will even have a drink. So what if it's morning? This is Calgary. Cowboy country. It will be his chance to toast his son to their new beginning.

"I'll have the steak and eggs, why not?" Mansoor says grandly.

"Yogurt and fruit for me."

"Is that all, son? Have something more substantial." Ashif needs to put on weight, build a more muscular physique. That's the only way other businessmen will take him seriously.

"I don't want anything heavy."

"Okay." Mansoor won't say anything now, but once Ashif is under his wing, he'll insist the boy start a healthier fitness and food regimen. Fit body, fit mind.

When the waiter leaves, Mansoor and Ashif exchange pleas-antries, like businessmen at the beginning of a meeting. They discuss the weather, the business news, yesterday's hockey game.

Mansoor taps the presentation on the chair next to him, waiting for an opening in their conversation, but it's Ashif who draws first. He reaches into his suit pocket and retrieves an envelope. "Here," he says, handing it to his father.

"What's this?" Mansoor takes the envelope with his name on the front. MR. MANSOOR VISRAM. He's impressed. His son is using "mister" to address him—clearly a sign of Ashif's growing respect for him.

"Open it," Ashif encourages him.

Mansoor slides a finger under the seal and lifts out a cheque in his name. An investment in the dry cleaners? What else could it be? The amount is exactly the amount he needs for his down payment. He laughs, shaking his head. "This is very generous but not necessary," he says. He didn't expect his son to invest money into their partnership. The family business was his birthright. He'd already booked an appointment with Abrahams & Abrahams. He is going to see them right after breakfast.

"I wanted to talk to you about . . ." Ashif starts.

"You won't believe it but I was thinking the same thing. How did you know I was going to ask you to join the business?"

"What? No, Pappa. That's not what this money is for."

Mansoor isn't listening. He's already set a copy of his business plan in front of Ashif. He taps the title page. "See that. We're going to revolutionize the retail industry, son. You and me together."

Ashif glances at the cover page. M.G. Visram & Son Dry Cleaners, Ltd. A Presentation to the City of Calgary. "A new business plan? That's what you need this money for?" His coffee cup rattles in its saucer.

"Everything will be automated, you see," Mansoor continues, unable to stop himself, after holding it in for what feels like a lifetime.

Ashif leans across the table and tries to stop him. "Look, Pappa. This is money so you can clear your debt and retire."

Mansoor reaches across and opens the business plan for Ashif. "We can take advantage of these new technologies, you see. Computers, the Internet, e-commerce," Mansoor continues undaunted. "It's the new frontier. But we've got to get in now. Before everyone else and their dog thinks it's a good idea, too. There's no time to waste."

"The Internet? Are you kidding? No one knows if dot-coms are a bubble or the real thing." Ashif taps his knife against his coffee cup. "You might as well be betting on horses."

Mansoor guffaws. As if his business was based on luck. It's based on mathematical models, on calculated risks. But Ashif should know that. He's a businessman. "Go ahead and check the numbers for yourself. Then you'll see."

Ashif slaps shut the business plan. "No more business plans for you, Pappa. It's too late now. The Internet is for young people."

Mansoor laughs. He flexes an arm over the table. "Feel this! I can do anything." Why does his son have such little faith in him? Mansoor has never let him down. Not once. Not ever. He's been an exemplary father. What's wrong with this boy?

Ashif sits back and clenches his knees.

"I'm stronger than most men your age. Fit body, fit mind."

"I want you to stop putting our family at risk. I also don't want Mummy to work anymore. She needs to retire, too."

Underneath the table, Mansoor knits his hands together. So what if Layla works? It's not as if her income is supporting the family. He had only asked her to contribute a little, that's all. Why was his son being so old-fashioned? "I'm sure she doesn't mind. It's like her *seva* to the community. Her service to all the young people who don't have home-cooked meals anymore."

Ashif feels his pulse in his fingertips, thinking about his mother's hands. "Not everyone is cut out for business."

"Absolutely true, not everyone is. I have told her, expand. People love her food. But she doesn't want to. And I don't like to pressurize anyone. Yet how much money can she make? White people, they love exotic foods. Just like in Uganda. Give them any kind of curry—Goan, Gujarati, Punj—"

"No, Pappa!" Ashif balls his fists on the table. "I'm talking about you. *You* are the one who's not cut out for business. Please just stop. For your sake and ours, too."

Mansoor slaps the table. "How dare you talk to me—"

"Here you go," the waiter says, sliding their orders in front of them.

Mansoor and Ashif fall silent. They gape at the food as if failing to understand what is expected of them.

"Can I get you anything else?" the waiter asks.

"We're fine, thanks." Ashif pushes his bowl of granola and

yogurt away. He leans forward and tries a new tact. "Look, Pappa. I know you've tried. We all do. You don't have to worry—I'm here. I'll take care of you and Mummy. This cheque is only your first instalment. I will support you. I want to," he says, trying to convince his father, himself too.

His son has some middle-management job, and he thinks he owns the world. As if *Mansoor* needs *his* money. "What about your promotion? Have you got it yet?" Mansoor shoves a piece of steak into his mouth and chews vigorously. Thirty-eight dollars for this? A complete waste of money.

Ashif sits back in his chair and lets out a sigh. "Not yet, but I will."

"Maybe they are considering you for a layoff?" Mansoor slides the cheque across the table to Ashif.

"I'm one of their top employees, Pappa. How many times do I have to tell you that?" Ashif half yells, unable to hold back his anger.

Two men at another table turn to look at them.

"Keep your voice down!" Mansoor says, motioning to the other tables with his knife. "We are not in some low-class place. What will people think?"

"I don't care what they think." Ashif sinks his spoon into the granola.

Ashif's outburst only reconfirms Mansoor's thoughts. His son will get laid off. No question about it. No one wants an employee who can't control himself. He reminds himself why they're here today: he needs to save his boy. "Quit, son! Come join me. Together we are unbeatable." He then hands Ashif the silver-plated business-card holder. "Go ahead, open it," he says with a broad smile.

Ashif pulls out a slip of card stock, a mocked-up business card in his father's handwriting. ASHIF M. VISRAM, B.COMM. (WITH DISTINCTION), *SHAREHOLDER & PARTNER*, M.G. VISRAM & SON DRY CLEANERS, LTD. He throws the paper and card holder down. "I'm not going to join the business, Pappa. Not now. Not ever. Get that through your head." He slides the cheque to his father. "This is your first instalment. But you will not, I repeat, use this money or any future money I send you for this business or any other business. You understand?"

Mansoor refuses the cheque with a shake of his head.

"This isn't a game, Pappa! You need to stop thinking about yourself. Think about us for once."

Mansoor is perplexed by his son's words. Think about them? That's all he does. His whole life is about them. His family. There is no difference for him between who he is and who they are. "Everything is for you...."

Ashif laughs. "For me? No, everything is for you." Then words spew out of him, like a volcanic eruption. "I hate my job, did you know that, Pappa? I can't stand it, actually. But why do I stay? Because of you! You can't take care of Mummy, so I have to. I want you to stop putting my mother's life in jeopardy!"

Mansoor turns his gaze outside. Rows of planes sit on the tarmac, like giant, motionless birds. His hands throb with pain as if they are bruised, as if his fingers are broken. He pumps his fists open and closed, but there is no relief.

Ashif tucks the cheque between the salt and pepper shakers. "The next time I speak to you, I only want to hear that you've sold the business, paid off the debt, and you're ready to retire. Understand me?" He stands up.

"Where are you going? There's still so much I want to tell you." Mansoor offers his son a copy of his plan. "It will change everything. Revolutionize the retail industry. I promise you."

Ashif shoos his father's hand away. "No more pipe dreams, Pappa. Enough is enough!" He buttons his jacket and briskly walks away.

Chapter 13

"ENOUGH IS ENOUGH," MANSOOR'S father said as he pushed open the front door with his cane. He was home for lunch, as always. Dwarfed behind him was his accountant, Badur, who carried a small brown bag stained with oil. A canvas bag hung from his shoulder. In his shirt pocket, a pocket-protector lined with pens; behind it, a pair of scissors, only the curved black handle visible. Mansoor was three years old. He sat at the dining table, his head resting on an outstretched arm, rolling a wooden toy car back and forth across the surface. His ayah, Jocelyn, sat next to him in a pinafore patterned with acacia trees. When Govindji walked in, Jocelyn sat up to attention. So did Mansoor. He was eager to say hello, but he knew he had to wait for his father to address him first.

"What a nice surprise, Badur *bhai*. You've come for lunch," Mansoor's mother, Gulzar, said. She was standing at the stove and quickly lifted her pacheri-scarf from around her neck to cover her head. "Let me bring another plate."

"No, no, *Bhai*. I am not eating," Badur said, shoving his Coke-bottle glasses up his nose.

"What have you come for then?" Gulzar asked.

Badur shifted his eyes to Govindji, who was already at the coal stove, lifting the lids on the pots.

"See what I mean, Badur *Bhai*? Vegetables again!" Govindji held a spoonful of cauliflower curry above the pot. "What are we? Paupers who can't afford meat? I can afford anything!" He threw the spoon back into the pot. It clanged against the side. "How's a man to live on vegetables alone? And look at my boy," he said, pointing to Mansoor. "Without a proper diet, how will he grow, *hanh*? Have I not provided everything for her, told her she can buy anything from the grocers, butchers, fishmongers, you name it? My only request: meat! Essential for the diet. Look at the Europeans, *hanh*? Solid. Rock solid. Meanwhile she wants my son to eat like a street boy. This is not India, lady. *This* is the new world. *This* is Africa!" Govindji shifted from one foot to the other as he jockeyed his pants up over his round belly.

"Give me the bag, Badur *Bhai*." Govindji waved his accountant forward.

Govindji pulled a chicken leg out of the bag and handed the bag back. He held the chicken leg to Gulzar's lips. "Eat," he commanded.

Gulzar leaned away from her husband.

Mansoor's small body stiffened.

Govindji took Gulzar by the base of her neck and pushed her lips to the chicken. "Open, I say."

Gulzar squirmed, frantically moving her head from side to side, her lips firmly pressed together. Piri-piri sauce dripped red down her chin.

Govindji dug his fingers into her mouth and pried it open. He tried to shove the chicken leg in.

Gulzar bit his finger instead.

The chicken leg fell to the ground.

Govindji's arm shot out. Gulzar's head snapped back.

"Animal!" he shouted.

Mansoor wrapped his arms around himself as if to keep from falling apart.

"What's a man to do with a woman like her, Badur *Bhai*?" Govindji kicked the chicken leg out of his way and turned to his accountant.

Badur handed Govindji a handkerchief.

"Defiant to the core!" Govindji pulled each greasy finger through the handkerchief. "I'm sick of it. Sick of her. Tells me she can't stomach it. But we are not Hindus anymore! How many times can I tell her? We don't believe in those hoodoo-voodoo ways anymore. Before we were Hindus, we were monkeys, so does that mean we should go back to eating bananas and walking on all fours, too?" Govindji chortled. "I say, Badur *Bhai*, you can take the girl out of the jungle but you cannot take the jungle out of her."

Gulzar continued preparing lunch, one side of her face bright red.

"Believe you me, I've done my level best to bring her into

the modern age. To educate her. You've got to change with the times. Otherwise you go the way of the dodo bird. But she's got stones up here," Govindji said, tapping his forehead. "You saw, didn't you, Badur *Bhai*? She is impossible."

"Yes, sir, I saw everything."

"Like trying to free a caged bird that refuses to fly. No man can manage a woman like her, that is for certain. And it is not just her inability to cook properly, you see. There is a long list of other infractions: she won't use toilet paper, she doesn't know how to use a fork and knife, and worse still, she wears this." Govindji tugged at Gulzar's pacheri-scarf. "I have even tried to enlist the help of a missionary. Imagine *me* asking a missionary for *his* help. I thought perhaps a religious angle would help. Not that I . . ." he glanced back as if to check that no one was listening ". . . am a believer. But the women, they often are. They love religion, superstition. That sort of hullabaloo. See that," he said, pointing to a framed photograph of the Aga Khan with his new European wife dressed in a pantsuit, the words WEAR SIMPLE COLONIAL DRESS followed by his signature printed beneath the photo. "The missionary gifted it to her, you see. You would think that would have made a difference. Nothing doing. Stubborn as a mule. Am I asking her to wear pants? Of course not! But some form of civility, please. What will people think, *hanh*? That I, Visram Popat Govindji, am married to some kind of savage? That *I* am some kind of backward fool? I even bought her a nice dress during a business trip to London. The latest fashion, I tell you. And what did she do with it? Added fabric to the bottom, turned it into a long dress, even extended the sleeves! I say, no gratitude in this woman whatsoever. Not one iota. In this, the European man has a clear advantage over us, Badur *Bhai*. Their women are educated, you see. They have class. Very good for business. The womenfolk chit-chat about this and that while the men discuss business. It is a perfect set-up. Your opponent lets down his guard at a social event—good food and drink in hand—thinking it is just a friendly gathering, when the main point is to a strike a deal. Imagine taking that," Govindji pointed to Gulzar, "to a dinner party or a business luncheon!"

"Difficult, sir, very difficult."

"No, this is unacceptable. A man of my position having a wife like her. Why can't she adjust herself, *hanh*? Is this not a feminine trait? But she's missing it—not just a little but *kabisa*. Something's wrong with her, Badur *Bhai*. Something is off in her genetic makeup. This is the peril of ordering a bride, sight unseen. I trusted my agent. And therein was my number-one problem. I should have gone and checked for myself. Made sure I was not getting damaged goods. I specifically requested an adjustable woman. But the only way to get anything done properly is to take matters into your own hands. Isn't that right, Badur *Bhai*?"

"Absolutely right," Badur said, tucking his hands into his pants pockets.

"So what choice do I have, Badur *Bhai*? None whatsoever. I have the well-being of my son, my future progeny, to think of.

What I need is a modern bride, one who will help educate my children. Build a future. I say, I have given her plenty of time to change. To become a modern woman."

"True, sir, more than plenty."

"Enough is enough!" Govindji called Jocelyn and the maid, Nelly, forward. "As I told you . . ." he said to them in Swahili.

The women flanked Gulzar, each one grabbing her by the wrist.

"What are you doing?" Gulzar said, trying to wriggle out of their grip.

They pulled her to the middle of the kitchen where Badur had already started laying newspaper on the floor.

Govindji lifted a kitchen chair and arched it over the air to Gulzar. He placed it behind her knees, then forced her down by her shoulders.

The women dropped down to the floor, one on each side of the chair. They pulled on Gulzar's wrists and buckled her down.

"Okay, Badur *Bhai*. You can start."

Badur plucked Gulzar's scarf from her head and handed it to Nelly. He pulled her bun down. Bobby pins flew out like startled cockroaches and skittered over the floor. Gulzar's thick black hair unravelled over her shoulders and down her back like a waterfall.

Badur removed the scissors from his shirt pocket.

Gulzar flip-flopped in the chair like a fish out of water.

"If you resist," Govindji said, "how will Badur *Bhai* do his job, *hanh*? You'll be scarred. And there's no point in scarring such a beautiful face," he said, running the back of his fingers over her cheek.

"Why are you doing this? Please, don't," Gulzar begged.

"It is your own fault, can't you see? Who asked you to be so stubborn? You are the one who wants to go back to India. So who am I to stop you? I will grant you your wish."

"Send me back? But what will they say?" Gulzar began to cry.

"Aye-ya-ya. No need to cry. I am doing this for your own good." Govindji then turned to his accountant. "Begin, Badur *Bhai*."

Mansoor cupped his hands over his face. "Mamma," he whispered into his palms, rocking back and forth. "Mamma."

The sound of scissors clipping in a frenzy filled the kitchen.

"Excellent work, Badur *Bhai*," Govindji said when the sound stopped.

Mansoor opened his eyes to see his father standing by the chair, the accountant wiping the scissors clean with a towel. A carpet of hair surrounded the chair. Jocelyn brushed hair off her cheek. Nelly wiped the back of her wrist across her lips.

"Now they will believe you," Govindji tapped Gulzar's head, her hair shorn to the scalp in the custom of widows. "I've done you a favour, can't you see? You can tell them I am dead. You are a widow and that is the reason you are back."

"Anything else, sir?" Badur asked.

"Just the papers."

"Right-right, sir."

"Please, can I hold my son?" Gulzar asked, her hands folded in a lap of hair.

"Yes, of course." Govindji turned to Mansoor. "Go to your mother."

"Come to me, *babu*," Gulzar said, her arms outstretched, her voice breaking.

But Mansoor did not recognize the person in the chair. Where was his mother? He scanned the room frantically, his eyes darting from face to face, looking for her. She had vanished. In her place: a man in his mother's dress. The image terrified him.

"Go, son." Govindji lifted Mansoor off his chair and placed him on the floor. "Go say goodbye to your mother." He pushed him forward.

Mansoor ran to his ayah.

Badur removed an ink pad and a set of forms from his canvas bag and smoothed them out on the kitchen table. Nelly held Gulzar by the elbow and helped her to the table like a nurse escorting a patient after surgery. Badur lifted Gulzar's hand, which hung limp in his. He pressed her thumb to the ink pad, then pushed it down on the port papers.

Later that day, Badur accompanied Gulzar on a train to Mombasa where he ensured she boarded the SS *Bombay*, reversing the trip she had made across the ocean four years earlier. Soon after the ship set sail, Gulzar jumped overboard and drowned. "That's too bad," Govindji said when he was told the news. "She was a good woman."

Weeks later, a new wife arrived, this time hand-picked by Govindji himself, this time from Uganda. She was fifteen years old.

"This is your new mummy," his father said. "Say hello."

Mansoor stuck his thumb in his mouth instead. He wanted his mummy. The real mummy. Where was his real mummy?

His father yanked his son's tiny wrist away from his mouth and held it up to his new wife. "Say hello or else!"

"Hello," Mansoor whimpered and shook the girl's hand.

"Anything else?" the waiter asks Mansoor.

It takes Mansoor a second to hear him, to reorient himself. He looks down at his half-eaten steak. Across the table, a bowl of granola and yogurt, hardly touched. "Just the bill."

"Your son has already taken care of it," the waiter says with a wink.

"No, no. I will pay." Mansoor fumbles. His fists are wrapped in napkins, like bandages. He casts them off and they fall to the floor. He roots through his wallet, hands the waiter a credit card.

"But it's already been paid for, sir." The waiter hands the card back.

Mansoor refuses to take the card. "There has been some sort of mistake. This card is good."

"It was a pleasure serving you, sir." The waiter puts the card down on the table. "We hope to see you again soon." He picks up Mansoor's plate and leaves.

Mansoor puts his card back into his wallet. He gathers up both copies of his presentation, the two calculators, the two pens, the silver-plated business-card holder. With trembling hands, he drops them back into his briefcase. He leaves the cheque with his name on it where Ashif had put it, between the salt and pepper shakers. He weaves through the tables of businessmen. It's the host who finally stops him from circling the lounge. He points him toward the elevator.

"That way down, sir."

PART TWO

Chapter 14

LAYLA ARRIVES AT JAMATKHANA with Shamma and Almas for the Night of Power on the northeast Calgary Ismaili mini-bus, which brings community members, mostly seniors, to and from jamatkhana for their morning and evening prayers. She tucks her chin to her chest, against the cold wind, and shuffles to the entrance of the prayer hall. She wishes Mansoor would come to jamatkhana with her. It would give him some peace of mind. But he hasn't been in years, decades even. She recently suggested that he should at least come tonight. "Lailatul Qadr is no ordinary night," she reminded him. "Our prayers tonight are equivalent to one thousand nights of prayer." Mansoor just laughed. "Sounds like Ali-Baba and One Thousand and One Arabian Nights!" he said. "What kind of a fool believes in that hocus-pocus?" Layla continued, undeterred. "It's the night Allah seals our fates for the coming year. We have to pray and ask for mercy and forgiveness." "Oh-ho, Layla. How many times can I tell you? Religion and story. They're one and the same thing. Fiction. All fiction."

The prayer hall is simple but elegant. The colours, too. Sandstone and cedar. The minarets are shaped like peaks instead of domes, an ode to the Rocky Mountains in the distant horizon. Soft lights cast a pale, soothing glow over the hall, which is full but not yet at capacity. Many more will arrive after evening prayers when the night formally begins at nine o'clock, and by midnight, the hall will be jam-packed with followers eager to take advantage of the night's most powerful prayers. The seniors sit at the back of the hall in chairs designated for them. The rest of the congregation sits on the carpet. Men on the right, women on the left. The leaders of the jamat-khana, two married couples, are on the carpet, too, but behind their *phats*, low tables at the front of the hall that face the congregation. Mukhi Sahib and Mukhiyani Ma, Kamadria and Kamariyani Ma. On their tables, a feast of offerings, including the platters of food Mukhiyani Ma ordered from Layla.

Close to midnight, Mukhi Sahib asks the congregation to stand for the midnight prayers. The congregation rises. Layla, too, her rosary beads in hand. A young woman with golden hair, dressed in a brilliant blue shalwar kameez, weaves through the congregation to the podium at the front of the hall. She turns to Mukhi. He nods. She presses her palms together in prayer and begins. *Ya Rahman, Ya Rahim. The Most Compassionate, the Most Merciful.* The congregation joins in, their voices building, like a wave, louder and louder, until they are swimming in sound.

Some leave after the midnight *tasbih* ends at one. Volunteers in their smart blue uniforms parcel out cashews and coffee beans to help those who remain stay awake. The night is spent with prayers interspersed with breaks, devotional songs, and *waez*-speeches from missionaries. By now, some have stretched out their legs, covering their feet with shawls. Others have their children at their sides, fast asleep under blankets. At four, the lights are dimmed and the congregation begins a silent meditation followed by regular morning prayers at five. Then, breakfast is served in the social hall. Some don't stay for breakfast, eager to get home to sleep or to get to work. Layla sits with the seniors, dunking *mumri* into cups of steaming chai. When they finish, they begin their procession to the jamati bus.

Snow swirls around the lampposts of the jamatkhana parking lot. In the distance, across Deerfoot Trail, the red light at the top of the Calgary Tower blinks on and off, like a lighthouse in a dark sea. Their bus driver, Al-Karim, who is a member of the Volunteer Corps, stands at the steps of the bus and offers his hand to those who need it. "Work, No Words." That's their motto. The Corps do so much good *seva*-service for the community, but they never tout their virtues to the world like a salesman hawking a product. God is watching, and that is enough. Once everyone is inside, Layla asks Al-Karim to help her with her cellphone. She'd noticed a message on it but didn't know how to retrieve it. The phone was a gift from Ashif after he bought a new one for himself. He insists that she use it whenever she wants. Call long distance. Call anyone you want.

But she keeps it for emergency purposes only. She does not want to waste her son's hard-earned money. Besides, she doesn't know how to use all the features, even though he had explained them to her. But how many new things can you learn in one lifetime?

"Of course." Al-Karim dials into her voicemail for her then hands the phone to her.

She hopes it is Ashif who's called. Maybe his plans have changed and he's coming home again? Or maybe he wants to tell her how his breakfast with his father went yesterday.

A woman's voice booms into her ear. "Hello, this is Sunnydale Hospital. We're sorry to leave this as a message. We're calling to inform you that Mansoor Visram was admitted to Emergency at four this morning. When you come to the hospital, please check in with Patient Services on the main level. Thank you."

The word *emergency* shatters in her mind like an icicle. She drops the phone. It clangs onto the bus floor. She feels dizzy. "Ashif," she says, as if that is enough to summon him.

Al-Karim retrieves the phone and listens to the message. "Don't worry, Aunty," he says, cupping her shoulder. "I'll take you. Arzeen works at that hospital. I'll ask her to meet us."

She nods but her instinct is to call Ashif. She takes her phone from Al-Karim and starts to dial and then stops. She shouldn't worry him uselessly. She will wait to find out what's happened to Mansoor first. *Please, Mowla, let my husband be okay.*

The seniors file through the hospital's revolving doors like schoolchildren through a turnstile. Layla tried to protest, but they insisted on keeping her company. "*Vando-nye*," she told them. "I'll be all right." Shamma and Almas were with her. "No, no, mustn't be alone," one senior said, resting her hand on Layla's shoulder from the seat behind, her fingertips stained with henna.

"Yes, exactly," another senior added. "Strength in numbers."

The seniors follow Al-Karim down a brightly lit corridor toward the hospital registration desk where Al-Karim's wife, Arzeen, is waiting for them in green scrubs, the baggy top hiding the roundness of her pregnant belly. She waves at Al-Karim. "Hey, babe," she mouths. He waves from the back of the group.

"*Ya ali madad*, Aunty." She embraces Layla as far as her stomach allows and kisses her on each cheek. "Everything will be okay," she whispers.

"*Inshallah*." Layla clutches her bag. "What has happened to Uncle?"

"We don't know yet, Aunty. We need to wait for the doctor."

"Is Dr. Murji here?" Layla asks, hoping for an Ismaili doctor. Not that she knows him personally. But he is the vice-chair of the Ismailia Health Care Board, and, as part of his duties, he gives speeches at all the jamatkhanas on health issues affecting the community.

"No, Aunty. I wish he was working today, too. Another doctor will meet us soon." Arzeen waves the group forward; her wedding ring glitters on her small hand. "Hullo, *vinjay*. Let's go," she says enthusiastically, as if she's leading a tour.

The waiting room looks like a seashell with its long curved wall that separates it from the hallway. Pumpkin-coloured chairs circle the room. It is empty except for an old Sikh man who is lying down across three chairs. He unhooks his arm from over his eyes and looks up at them for a second before returning to his original position on his makeshift bed.

Community members settle in, taking up most of the chairs. Shamma removes a plate of *tepla* from her bag of *naandi,* the daily auction of food offerings at jamatkhana, and passes it around. Without being asked, Al-Karim takes orders for tea.

"Tim Hortons? *Shabash*. Would have brought a Thermos of chai from home had we known," a senior says, shaking her head. All the seniors request double-doubles.

The sound of the large clock on the wall is a heartbeat that gets louder and louder until it feels like a pulse in Layla's ears. She retrieves her cellphone from her handbag and wraps her fingers tightly around it. As she waits for news from the doctor, she thinks of the last time she saw Mansoor. Yesterday morning, on his way to breakfast with Ashif. He was in such good spirits. What happened to him after?

The attending emergency physician, a young man with dishevelled red-blond hair and a stethoscope folded into his jacket pocket, stands at the front of the waiting room. He holds a file splayed open in his hands. "Mrs. Visram?"

Arzeen holds Layla by the elbow as they follow Dr. Poole down a long corridor toward a room with the sign QUIET ROOM B. Why do they call it the Quiet Room? Is it to encourage people to keep their emotions in, silence themselves when they are being told the news? All Layla wants to do is to scream so loudly that her son will hear her.

The doctor holds the door open with an outstretched arm. Inside, there is a small white table with several chairs around it. Layla sits down, cradling her handbag in her lap. She places a palm over the bulge of her cellphone. Arzeen stands next to her, like a guard, her hand on Layla's shoulder.

"Mrs. Visram, let me explain what has happened to your husband," the doctor says as he pulls a chair next to her. "We're not quite sure of the circumstances that led to his injuries, but we know that he must have been outside for quite an extensive period in these temperatures. He's suffered from severe hypothermia. He wasn't wearing proper clothing. He's very lucky that he was found."

"Outside?" Layla asks, puzzled.

"Yes. He was found in a farm field near Airdrie."

"But he was supposed to be at the business. He is always at the business," she says, her eyebrows knitted together. "What was he doing in Airdrie?"

"I'm sorry. I'm not sure of the details. The police will have them. They should be arriving soon. It will be a part of their investigation. But what I can tell you about is your husband's health."

Layla nods. The word *investigation* makes her nervous. She squeezes her cellphone more firmly.

"We've had to intubate your husband." Dr. Poole rests both palms on the table. "Let me explain what that means. At some point your husband lost his ability to breathe on his own. This can happen when a body is traumatized. The body literally shuts down. Blood rushes away from non-vital organs and goes immediately to life-sustaining ones. The heart. The lungs. That's actually a good thing, which probably sounds funny. But what happens is that our instinct for survival kicks in."

Layla silently begins calling the names of the Imams. Mawlana Ali, Mawlana Hussein, Mawlana Zayn al-Abidin, Mawlana Muhammad al-Baqir.

"He didn't have any vitals when he was found. But the good news is that we were able to resuscitate him in the ambulance. That's the miracle of the technology we have today. They inserted a tube into his throat which was then hooked up to a ventilator. It's this machine that breathes for him. . . ."

Layla can barely hear the doctor. She hears the words CT scan, x-ray, blood pressure, but his voice is a distant echo. Her prayers are roaring in her mind. *YA ALI. YA ALI. YA ALI.* It's only when the doctor reaches over and gently touches her arm that she hears him again.

"Mrs. Visram, from what we can see, your husband has not sustained any bodily injuries with the exception of a laceration on his left leg and frostbite on several toes and fingers. But that's nothing to worry about. We're taking care of that. But what we can't be sure of is if he has sustained any internal injuries. That's our first priority. We need to run some tests to find out, but unfortunately we can't do that until his body warms up."

The doctor goes on to explain the process of rewarming. He speaks about blankets, a machine that blows hot air over Mansoor's body, warm fluid IVs, and bladder flushes.

Layla imagines Mansoor encased in ice. She is not interested in the doctor's technical details. She just wants to know that her husband will be all right. "When will he be unfrozen?"

"If you're asking about rewarming, the times vary. It could be a couple of hours or the better part of a day or longer. Your husband's core temperature fell to dangerous levels. Maybe you'd like to see him now?"

"No." Layla's hands begin to tremble. She does not want to see her husband the way the doctor has described him, like some kind of machine. "I will see him with my son."

"Will he be here soon?"

"I hope so."

"Okay." Dr. Poole pushes his chair back. "As soon as we know anything, you'll be the first to hear."

Outside the Quiet Room, Layla pulls out her cellphone. She presses on the number one, her hands still trembling. The phone makes a sing-song of sounds as it dials Ashif's number. She is relieved to hear her son's voice on the other end of the receiver. She wells up with tears and is about to say something when she realizes that it is only his voicemail. "Hey, you've reached Ash. You know the drill." Where is Ashif? She hopes he hasn't left for Vancouver already. She leaves him a brief message and asks him to return her call, though she knows he will not like this message. "Be clear, Mummy. You know how busy I am. I need to know what you're calling for. Don't just say, call me. Give me specifics."

"Okay, *bheta*," Layla had said, but she is stifled by this requirement. Often there are no details to give. She is only calling to say hello, to inquire on how he is, to hear his voice. So she tries to limit the calls she makes to him. She does not want to disturb him. Instead, she waits for him to call her, just as she will now.

Chapter 15

WHEN ASHIF FINALLY CALLS his mother, it's past eight in the morning and he's checking out of his hotel in Calgary. He has two employee meetings this morning before he leaves for Vancouver. He'd seen her missed calls. One from yesterday and one today. But neither message said anything. Just, "call me."

"But that makes no sense, Mummy," Ashif says to his mother, adjusting his tie. "A farm field?"

"Yes," Layla says loudly as if she is speaking to someone overseas. "Near Airdrie."

"Is he all right?"

"I don't know."

"What do you mean, you don't know?" he asks curtly. "Didn't you ask the doctor?"

"Yes."

"And what did he say?"

"They are thawing him out."

"Sorry?" He presses his thumb to his ear.

"Defrost," Layla says loudly.

"You mean frostbite?" he offers.

"The doctor said frostbite."

"Okay, good. So he's okay." He's relieved that his father's injuries are minor. Once, when he was a child, he had frostbite. He had forgotten his gloves and toque at home. He just tucked his hands into his winter jacket, but there was no way to protect his head from the icy temperature. After recess, his ears were red and raw and he was sure they would fall off. The school nurse treated him for frostbite and sent a note home with him listing appropriate winter clothing and stores where they could be purchased. If needed, the school could pay for the items. Layla tore up the note and made him promise not to tell his father. He didn't. Ashif asked her to sew his gloves to his coat, like the other kids, and she did.

"What else did the doctor say?" he asks briskly, trying to get his mother to get to the point. He checks his watch. He has a flight to catch.

"They will do some tests," Layla continues, "but not until he has finished thawing out."

"But thawing doesn't make sense, Mummy!" he says, his frustration growing. He can't tell if his mother is withholding information to prevent him from worrying or if she hadn't understood what the doctors told her. Or maybe she hadn't asked any questions, deferring, as she always did, to authority whether it was a doctor, a police officer, or his father. He holds the receiver between his shoulder and chin and slips off his suit jacket. "What does Pappa say?"

"Nothing. I have not seen him yet."

"I'm calling the hospital right now," Ashif says firmly, like a teacher reprimanding a child.

"But I don't want to see him without you, *bheta*. Please come," Layla says, now crying.

Ashif suddenly feels guilty for being harsh with his mother. The same feeling of sinking into quicksand. "Everything will be okay, Mummy," he says. He reminds himself she has no one else she can count on. Just him. "I'll be there soon."

When he hangs up, he tells Mel that he needs to leave after their morning meetings to take care of a family matter. He then asks her to handle the first few meetings in Vancouver without him. She agrees and he rebooks himself on the next flight out.

Chapter 16

MANSOOR TUCKS A STACK of bills and rolled coins into a bank bag. It's only seven-thirty in the evening. A little early to be cashing out, but he's eager to get home tonight and tell Layla his news even if he's not sure she'll fully understand its importance. That doesn't matter to him. He has a great need to say it out loud. Tell someone. He reaches into his shirt pocket and removes the faxed letter that arrived an hour ago. He slips on his bifocals and reads it yet again. "Yes-yes-yes!" Abrahams & Abrahams approved his mortgage. Just like that. The interest rate is higher, but what does it matter? He can finally buy his plant, show the City his power.

He retrieves his cellphone from his pants pocket and tries Ashif again. That's who he really wants to tell. Now his son will believe him. Not doubt him as he did this morning at breakfast. "I'm on my way up, son!" What a difference a day makes. The phone makes a sing-song of sounds and soon, he gets the same voice recording. "We're sorry, you have reached a number that has been disconnected or is no longer in service."

Mansoor shakes his head. Why didn't Ashif give him his new number? He'll call his son when he gets home. Layla will have the right number, no doubt.

He collects his winter coat and briefcase from the backroom. At the front of the store, he catches a glimpse of himself in the glass door. He throws a punch at the faint image. "Look at you now, Visram!" Another punch. "You were right all along, weren't you?" He flips the OPEN sign over to CLOSED, turns off the lights, and steps out of his store.

Mansoor and his boss stood at the back of a massive showroom. Outside, a neon sign blinked on and off. PATTERSON USED CARS & TRUCKS. Behind them, plaques with a photograph of a salesman and a bronze plate engraved with a name and month. The Salesman of the Month Award. The Wall of Fame. Mansoor's face appeared, again and again, under years 1973 to 1979.

"Come on now, Manny, if you want to see these," his boss said, tilting his head toward the wall, "then don't quit on me." He was a large man with a boyish face.

"I'll bring the plaques back, Fred." Mansoor slapped Patterson on his shoulder. "Since when have I let you down?"

"I'm losing my best man. You can't expect me to be happy about it."

"I understand," Mansoor said. But there was no turning back. He had joined Patterson Used Cars & Trucks almost as soon as he arrived in Canada. The job was commission-based, which appealed to him. He was paid on performance, not a salary for merely clocking in. It was as close as a job could get to being like a business. But in the end, it was still just a job. He was just an employee. He had a boss to answer to and there was no way Mansoor could have tolerated that for much longer. Working here had always been a temporary venture. Only until he had enough money to put a down payment on his own business. Business was the only way. The only way to own land, to call something your own, and rebuild the family legacy.

It had taken five years of working day and night, weekends, too, keeping a tight control on spending, to finally amass the funds he needed. He then spent the past year combing the province on evenings and his days off in search of the right opportunity. He'd been outbid on three promising operations. Then last month, he closed a deal on a gas station. It was located on an empty stretch of highway between Rocky Mountain House and Red Deer, two hours north of Calgary, making it a primary stop for truckers and oilmen on their way to a work site, construction workers from nearby projects, tourists and campers on their way to the Icefields Parkway, or motorists caught in a snowstorm. But he had no plans to move the family there. He wasn't confident that he'd be able to find Ashif a good school in such a small town and a proper education for his son was imperative. It had been hard enough to get him a place at Calgary's best public school. Besides, it was a temporary matter. Once the gas station was on solid ground, he would hire a manager to run it and expand with a second location, closer to home.

"If you ever decide to come back, Manny, there'll always be a spot for you here." Patterson tucked his thumbs under his suspenders. "Business is a tough proposition, after all."

"Thanks, Fred." Mansoor loosened his tie. This idiot should be working for him, not the other way around. He had more business acumen in his pinky finger than his boss had in his whole body.

"So, what you gonna do with all these plaques? Sell them?" Patterson chuckled.

Mansoor laughed along. "I just want to take some photos at home with the family. For the sake of posterity, you know? Don't want to forget these years."

"Well, it's quite an accomplishment. Just bring them back, okay?" Patterson said and started for his office.

"Absolutely. First thing." Mansoor stepped onto the ladder and reached up for a plaque with his name.

Soon, the accountant, Patel, a slight man with greasy hair, walked up. "Just finished lunch," he said in Gujarati, pulling the fingers of his right hand through a handkerchief. "Let me help you, brother."

"English, please!" Mansoor ordered in a sharp whisper as he handed him a plaque. One of Patel's brothers was the janitor here and another, a junior salesman. The brothers often lunched together in the backroom, bringing tiffins of curries from home. The insides of their lockers were tiny altars adorned with bronze

Ganeshas and incense sticks. They performed *poojas* there and unabashedly continued their day with red-and-yellow markings on their foreheads. Mansoor complained to Patterson about it, saying it would chase customers away. But Patterson said it didn't matter. Most of them were just back-office staff. No one would see them anyway. But that was beside the point. Mansoor would still have to see them.

When he was done, Mansoor weaved through the cars to the front of the showroom. Patel followed with the box of plaques like a lackey. Mansoor's colleagues gathered like penguins in their dark suits and white shirts, marching in formation, to say goodbye. Some patted him on the back and wished him luck, others shook his hand and congratulated him. But he knew that most of them were happy to see him go. No more competition.

"Stop wasting your time with goodbyes," Patterson said, popping his head out from his office. "He's coming back with the plaques tomorrow."

On his way home, Mansoor stopped at Marlborough Mall and pulled in front of a row of Dumpsters at the back of the building. He unloaded the boxes from his trunk, hoisted each one up and into the bin. The plaques clanged against the metal before landing on the pile of garbage. Wall of Shame, more like it! His good name was now permanently erased from that low place. As if he had never worked there. The money he saved there had been converted, like money at a foreign exchange, into his new business. He was starting his real life, the one he was supposed to be living.

Mansoor treads across the icy parking lot to the far end of the plaza, where he unlocks the bank's night deposit vault and drops the canvas bag of his day's earnings inside. He decides to buy a bottle of champagne on the way home. Yes, why not? Layla doesn't drink, but maybe tonight she'll have a sip. She's done it before. An image comes to him of her taking a sip of his whisky at a party then scrunching up her face before spitting it out. He laughed then as he does now. Better buy a bottle of non-alcoholic champagne, too. He doesn't want to drink alone.

Chapter 17

AT THE HOSPITAL, ARZEEN informs Layla and the growing number of community members that the medical staff have started a series of internal tests. The results will be available soon. Mansoor's body has responded well to the rewarming regiment.

"You doctors are top class," a senior says, tipping his fedora to Arzeen.

"She's not a doctor," Almas whispers.

"She can be my doctor anytime," he says with a wink to Arzeen.

Arzeen shakes her head and turns away.

"Our prayers are working," another senior says, clenching her prayer beads to the ceiling.

"Let's get the test results first," Arzeen cautions.

"True, but it can't be a bad sign, no, that his body is waking up like this?" the senior adds.

"True." Arzeen sits down between Layla and Shamma.

After more and more people arrive, Arzeen arranges for the

group to move from the waiting room to a family room. "We'll be more comfortable in here," she says to Layla, making Layla even more thankful for the girl's constant presence today. The room is a rectangle, like a small hall. It has three pea-coloured couches and padded folding chairs, some of which are clustered into small groups. The door to an adjoining room, an extension to the main room, is held open with a chair that is stacked with winter jackets. The smaller room is also filled with people from the community, many holding paper plates filled with snacks brought by the constant flow of visitors. Aluminum platters of *nylon-bhajia*, potato-*kachoori*, and chut-neys are spread on the tables of both rooms along with boxes of Timbits, used Tim Hortons cups, and dirty serviettes.

For the first time since Layla arrived at the hospital four hours ago, she feels that she can finally breathe. Soon, they will have some news.

"How many months, *dhikri*?" Shamma asks, rubbing Arzeen's belly.

"Seven months, Aunty," she replies, beaming. "I'm due at the end of April."

"How old are your twins now?" Shamma asks.

"The boys just turned three. I can't believe it."

"And this one?" Layla asks. "A boy or a girl?"

"A girl," she says, rubbing her belly, "and we couldn't be happier."

They tried for close to a year for a second child. Layla was sure she was too old. She was almost forty. Then the doctor gave them the news. She was pregnant. When Ashif found out, he begged her to have a boy. "No sisters!" Layla laughed. "It's not up to me, *bheta*. God will give us what he thinks we deserve."

She had done everything right, went to all her checkups, did everything the doctor said. At seven months, she had an appointment to see an ultrasound of the baby. But instead of the *boom-boom-boom* of her little girl's heartbeat, there was nothing. Her baby was dead.

The placenta had attached too deeply, the doctor explained. She would still have to deliver the baby. Layla did not remember taking the pills or being rushed into the operating room, though she did remember Mansoor's face as he ran beside the stretcher, his fingers clenched around the steel railing. She moaned and pushed until finally they had to cut her open and remove the baby. And all her womanly parts, too.

"Would you like to hold her for a bit?" a nurse offered.

Layla nodded. She pulled away the pink blanket, examined the baby's face, her tiny arms and legs, counted her fingers and her toes.

"When can we take her home?" Layla asked.

"I'm sorry, Mrs. Visram." The nurse reached for the baby. "I have to take her now."

"Please, I want to take her home."

The nurse tried again. Layla slapped her hand away. "No! She's mine."

"Please don't," Mansoor said to the nurse.

The nurse stepped aside.

"Layla, please," Mansoor said. "Give her to me."

"She needs a name!" Layla wept. "She can't be nameless. How else will Allah know who she is?" Her daughter had not been baptized. No one would baptize a dead child. She would not have an Ismaili burial. She was not Ismaili. This fact alone shattered Layla.

"What name do you like?" he asked.

"Maryam. I like Maryam."

"Okay." He took the baby from her. "Let me take care of our little Maryam."

When Mansoor came back, he told Layla he had taken care of everything. Their Maryam was at peace. He made sure of it. He also closed the gas station and made arrangements for Ashif's care. He stayed with Layla all day and insisted she eat when she refused. "You need your strength. Please—" he inched forward the bowl of soup on her food tray "—we all want you home."

"When are you coming back?" she asked. "We all want you home, too." It had been over four months since he had moved for the gas station.

"Soon. Very soon."

For a moment, her mind flashed to the camp in London. The endless agony of waiting for him. She wanted her husband at home by her side, by Ashif's side.

"I promise." He then handed her a soup spoon and she took it. "Listen, Layla. There's no disputing the science. The doctor showed me the graphs. It happens in eight-point-one percent of births."

But she refused to accept it. She had done something to deserve this fate. She was sure of it. God isn't unjust. He does not just dole out rewards and punishments randomly. Who would believe in a creator this cruel? There was a reason for everything. God is always watching and she must have made an error. She'd done something to anger him. But what? What had she done wrong?

Before Layla checked out of the hospital, the nurse gave her instructions on how to avoid mastitis. Don't express or use warm compresses. Never stand in a hot shower, no matter how painful her breasts were. It would only make things worse. The best way to stop her milk was cold compresses. Ice packs were a good option. So were iced cabbage leaves.

"You just have to be patient with yourself, dear," the nurse said as she helped Layla into her winter coat. "Our bodies just need a little time to understand."

For weeks after, Layla spent her days in bed with the curtains drawn. Shamma and Almas arrived with care packages of food. They visited daily, just as they would have if she had come home with a baby. Almas combed her hair; Shamma gave her manicures and pedicures. They took away the box of baby clothes Layla had knit and the toys people had gifted her, replacing them with games and books for Ashif. They played with him, took him out for ice cream. Anything to keep him occupied for Layla's sake, as well as his. He was eleven years old and they, like Layla, wanted to protect him from the news.

"Are you sick, Mummy?" Ashif asked when he came home from school and found her in bed with a bag of ice on each breast.

"My heart hurts, *bheta*," she said, pushing herself to sitting.

"'Cause of the baby?" Ashif asked, twisting the edge of his T-shirt around a finger.

"Yes."

His face fell. "I'm sorry."

"Come, *bheta*," she said, patting the edge of the bed.

He went to her.

"Don't worry," she said, cupping his face in her hands. "Mummy's okay."

He nodded, but she could sense he didn't believe her. He knew, like she knew, that she would never be okay again.

"You want to stay in my room?" she asked. "Until Pappa comes back home." If he was close to her, it would, she hoped, help alleviate his worry. Alleviate some of her sadness, too.

"But my toys are in my room."

"We can move into your room then, okay?"

He nodded.

She pulled him to her and wrapped her arms around his small body. "You are such a good boy. What would Mummy do without you?"

It was Shamma and Almas who suggested she enter the Silver Jubilee chicken samosa competition. "Everyone is doing it, Layla *Bai*," Shamma said. "Who doesn't want a chance to cook for the Imam?"

"It will give you some peace of mind," Almas added. Layla did not answer but she knew right away she would do it. This was her chance to reverse her fate, to clear her good name with the Almighty.

A new energy surged through her. Her days became singularly focused: making samosas. She refused visitors, reorganized her pantry, banned Ashif from the kitchen. She tested recipe after recipe. More garlic. Less clove. Chicken from Iqbal's. Better. She tried different methods for rolling the dough: water on the rolling pin, ghee on the rolling pin, roll in not out. She experimented for weeks, remembering the small tweaks and changes by heart. The smell of fried samosas settled into the house like a permanent guest.

She cried for days when she received the news. First place! She even cried while she made the samosas, an endless stream of tears dripping into the dough. She tried to stop herself but she just couldn't do it. It was only later that she realized that her tears were part of his great blessings: the Imam, as always, eats all our sorrows. This thought brought her so much relief she broke out into fits of laughter. She laughed so hard she cried. All praise is due to Allah! It was then that she made her vow. "I will never make my chicken samosas for anyone but the Imam." A secret pact. She promised Khudavind to hold the recipe for him, and him alone. In return, she asked him to please protect her son. Make sure no harm comes to the only child she and Mansoor would ever have.

Dr. Poole stands in the doorway of the family room, scanning the crowd of faces. He has several large brown envelopes tucked under his arm. "Mrs. Visram," he says, spotting Layla. "Can you come with me, please?"

Layla glances, yet again, at the clock. The fear she feels at the sight of the doctor quells with the thought of Ashif. He will be by her side soon.

Chapter 18

MANSOOR'S CAR IS PLUGGED into a low post, a tangle of extension cords, like the reins of a horse, heaped under the front bumper. When weighing all the options, the Chevy Impala always comes out on top.

He unplugs his car from the post and retrieves a snow brush from the back seat. He circles the car, occasionally patting it with a gloved hand as he brushes off the snow. Inside the car, he pulls out an organizer from the glove compartment. It folds open like a wallet. From one of the pockets, he removes a small black notebook with grid-lined paper. He flips on the light, checks the odometer reading, and scribbles the number under today's date. Not only was this a good way to monitor gas consumption and costs, he also used it as a formal record for tax writeoffs.

He reaches for the CD organizer on the passenger side floor and pulls a disc out. He holds it to the soft glow of the dashboard. *Kenny Rogers & Dolly Parton, Greatest Hits*. Mansoor enjoys all country music but this is one of his favourites. He loves Kenny's deep voice, his rhythm, his lyrics, many of which provide apt advice, not only on love, but on business, too. Kenny is a man's man. The best part of Kenny, of course, is that he often pairs himself with Dolly Parton. What a beauty! Mansoor knows all of her lyrics, too, from her earlier songs like "I Will Always Love You" to more recent hits like "Yellow Roses." Dolly moves like a doll on stage, a ballerina in a box, perfectly balancing her gorgeously imbalanced body. Her mass of golden hair, her rhinestone-tasseled blouses, her studded jackets. Mansoor can watch her for hours, in country music specials like *From Nashville with Love* and *The Queens of Country*. Dolly is, as far as he's concerned, the perfect woman. She gives you the feeling that you can hold her in your palm, like a bird, but she won't fly away over the smallest of difficulties. So much like Layla when he first met her. Whatever happened to that woman?

Mansoor had his choice of any woman he wanted. Not only did he come from one of Kampala's top families, but his father, unlike most fathers, gave him free rein to choose his bride rather than submit to a match. His only criteria was that the girl had to be from Africa—not India.

Applications started pouring in as soon as people heard. Parents sent their daughters' photographs along with a portfolio of personal qualities and skills. He made a short list of ten. Layla was one of them.

Mansoor crossed Lake Victoria by ferry, from Kampala to Kisumu, to meet her. Her family lived in a small two-room bungalow in the bustling city centre. It was clear they did not have much money, but he admired how well-kept the house was. Layla was even prettier than her pictures with her stunning ivory skin and high cheekbones. She was also, as promised, a superb cook. She had made a lunch of chicken *kalyo*, a creamy curry flavoured with saffron, that she served with hot chapattis and rice. He had three helpings. After lunch, he was allowed to accompany her on a walk along the beach, but only with an escort, her young cousin, Hanif.

They ambled along the crowded boardwalk until Layla suggested they try the beach. She clutched her dress each time a wave rolled in. Little Hanif trailed behind them, tossing stones into the waves. A large wave rolled in. Layla's feet sank into the sand, toppling her.

"Careful!" Mansoor reached down and pulled her up from her knees, but her dress was soaked, her makeup ruined.

"Let's go back," Mansoor offered.

"Why? Just give me your jacket."

He slipped off his jacket and placed it around her shoulders.

From her shell-shaped purse, she removed a compact mirror and some tissue. She snapped open the mirror and dabbed her eyes to remove the dripping lines of mascara. She reapplied her lipstick and adjusted a few bobby pins. All of that, right in front of him. Most girls (and he knew so many) would have insisted on going home or else they may have thrown a tantrum.

Not Layla. She adjusted calmly to a change in circumstances. No fuss at all. That's a sign of a grown woman. He wanted to kiss her, run his hands over the curves of her body. But he knew he couldn't. Not with a woman like Layla. There were rules he had to follow and he would. That afternoon, he asked her father for her hand, and to his delight, he agreed. Three months later, on their wedding night, he was finally allowed to touch her.

A tingling sensation radiates through Mansoor's legs and groin. But the feeling leaves as quickly as it arrives. It has been years since Layla had shared a bed with him or for that matter, even touched him. Since anyone had touched him. He pushes the CD into its socket and presses play. He shifts the car into drive and begins his long journey home.

On McKnight Boulevard, Mansoor glimpses the mountain-shaped minarets of Headquarters Jamatkhana. It's only now he remembers that it's the Night of Power. Layla won't be home, damn it. She'll be at the prayer hall all night. It's her duty she tells him—every *momin*'s duty—to attend jamatkhana on a daily basis, especially on such an auspicious night. But what about her duty to him as his wife?

He doesn't want to return to an empty house, especially not tonight. He should have stayed at the store, as he often does, folding open the cot, and watching TV, or else trying to finish the endless paperwork, until he's certain that Layla is home.

Not that Mansoor eats dinner with her—she has always eaten much earlier—or that he and Layla have much to say to each other. But at least when she is home, the house is filled with the everyday sounds of a house—a tap running, dishes being cleared away, the kettle whistling—and these sounds comfort him, especially after a long day at work.

He does not want to celebrate alone. But where can he go? "Should have come to jamatkhana with me," he can hear Layla say. "It will give you peace of mind." But does prayer put food on the table? Does it improve your business? Does prayer make your life easy? No, no, and no. There had been a time when he made an effort to go to jamatkhana—to make Layla happy. But he never found any solace at the prayer hall, just a deep sense of loneliness among the rows of men sitting cross-legged on the carpeted floor. Nothing bonded him to them. These men had simpler lives, he imagined. They had a God to praise when things went well, a God to blame when they didn't. Things were always out of their hands, and this kind of thinking he would never accept. Not that he would ever say it out loud. Of course not! Who wants to be ex-communicated? There were some things, his father wisely advised, that must be kept private. First and foremost, religion and politics. Safety in numbers.

If this were Uganda, he could have shown up at any number of establishments to find a friend and, more likely, a group of friends. No need to call ahead to make an appointment. He could have gone to City Bar, a smoke-filled café in the down-town core of Kampala, for a game of cards and a whisky, and if not there, then he would have gone to the local gymkhana to play badminton or to swim, followed by dinner and drinks at the Hilton, sometimes not getting home until the family was either fast asleep or just waking up in the morning. Back then, a man could find reprieve from the pressures of everyday life, from family and obligation. Men could be men, they could relax, drink, smoke, play cards without the nagging interference of a woman. Mansoor could have told any one of these men his news and they would have helped him celebrate.

His closest friends are now scattered around the world like pieces of a jigsaw puzzle. Tariq was in England; Fateh in Sweden; Kamru in Mozambique; Mohammed in Texas. Men he'd spent his life with, gone. Holes in his history like a book riddled with paper punches. He spoke to Mohammed now and then. But it was too costly to call often. Sometimes they wrote to each other. But it was never satisfying. You only got the broad strokes. There was no way to have a real conversation, to share the news of the day. Instead, you trailed behind each other's lives, learning what happened months earlier. Might as well be reading a history book. But maybe with the Internet, things will be different. Only recently, Mansoor read about something called search engines. Like having a worldwide encyclopedia at your fingertips. Imagine the possibilities! Maybe now he will be able to find his friends and connect with them on a regular basis. He hopes so.

He had hardly spoken to his sisters, either. But for different reasons. He had never been close to them. Not just because they were girls and so much younger than him, but also because he never considered them his real sisters. He had no interest in their company. Maybe if they lived here instead, he would have felt differently. Maybe then he would have joined forces with his brothers-in-law. But they had settled in Birmingham. Their fortunes from Uganda hadn't amounted to much, but enough to start a business. A movie rental store, which was now one of the biggest in the city.

A few blocks from home, Mansoor catches a green sign with a flashing beer mug. HARRY'S SPORTS BAR. It's not the kind of place he would normally go to, not that he really goes out. He would rather be in Canyon Creek, near his store, or any other professional neighbourhood than this one. You can't walk a bloody block here without seeing a sari or a turban. But he's too tired to drive all the way back to Canyon Creek. Not at this hour. Not when he's this close to home. He pulls his car in front of the sports bar, gathers his winter coat and briefcase, and steps out into the cold.

Chapter 19

AT THE ICU NURSING station, Ashif lays his briefcase on the counter and asks for his father's room. A nurse with black cat-eye glasses directs him to the family room. "Just down the hall, love," she says, pointing her pencil down a corridor. "They've been waiting for you."

Ashif stands at the entrance of the brightly lit family room and scans the crowd for his mother. He expected her to be alone, but the room and the one connected to it are both crowded with people from the community, rocking back and forth in unison, prayer beads in hand. *Ya Rahman, Ya Rahim. The Most Compassionate, the Most Merciful.*

"He's here!" a woman shouts, the first to spot him.

Eyes pop open, people turn toward him. A few let out extended sighs. "Thank God!"

"There she is, son." A man points to Layla, who is surrounded by a circle of women, including one he recognizes as Arzeen. She hasn't changed at all. She's still perfectly put together, her hair straight and coloured caramel-blonde.

Ashif smiles and waves. The crowd parts for him. When he reaches his mother, he sets his briefcase and suit carrier down and takes her in his arms.

Layla hands Arzeen her handbag. She wraps her hands around Ashif's arms and pulls herself to standing. She smells like rosewater.

"There's no need to cry anymore." He takes his mother in his arms. "I'm here now."

But she doesn't stop crying. She clutches onto Ashif. "We have to keep praying," she mumbles into his chest. "Set him free."

"Of course we're going to pray." He gently pushes her back. Her eyes are red and swollen: she must have been crying for hours. "Let's go and see him first, okay?"

"We can't," Layla says, her words barely audible. "He's gone."

"Where?" Ashif asks. "Another hospital?"

It's Arzeen who finally takes Ashif to the quiet room and tells him. His father passed away this morning. He was dead on arrival.

"What do you mean, dead on arrival?" He understands the term, but his mind deflects the idea, like a shield.

"We're not sure of the exact time of death, but we now know that he was already dead when the paramedics got to him."

"That makes no sense!" he says, practically shouting. "He was alive this morning." He is sure Arzeen is speaking about another patient. She's mixed up.

"Your father was on life support, Ash, so yes, he was alive in a sense. But neurologically, he was dead." She squeezes his hand.

"What are you saying? My father was half-dead, half-alive?" He pulls his hand away.

"I'm saying there's just no way to assess a cold body. You have to warm it up first before you can tell what's going on internally. That's normal protocol. And sometimes that requires reviving a patient if there are no vitals. And that's what we did with your father."

He imagines his father, lying on the hospital bed like frozen meat being warmed in a microwave. He gasps for air. The quiet room is shrinking. He throws back his chair, stumbles to standing. He can't breathe.

He slams open the door and rushes out into the hall. The antiseptic smell of the hospital assaults his nostrils. He starts to run to an exit sign. His legs buckle under him and in the middle of the hallway, Ashif falls to his knees.

When he's calm, Arzeen leads him back to the family room. Layla calls him to her. She's exactly as he left her: palms on her knees, a rosary pooled in her lap.

The room is so crowded now, he can barely push through. More people from the community arrive every minute. The seniors continue to pray, some silently, others out loud, all of them rocking back and forth in unison, pulling the beads of their *tasbihs* forward. A prayer to release his father's soul. His nose prickles with the smell of sandalwood incense.

"I want to see Pappa," Ashif says, walking toward Layla.

"You must be Ashif," a voice behind him says.

He turns to see a man about his age in a shiny grey suit and a pale yellow shirt, no tie.

"*Ya Ali Madad.*" He extends his hand to Ashif. "I'm Naushad Jivraj, convener of the Mayat and Ghusal Committee. And this—" he pats the man next to him, an older man with a Canadian flag and an Ismaili flag pinned at diagonals on his tie "—is Shamshu Bhai, my vice-convener."

Shamshu Bhai shakes Ashif's hand, too. "Take a seat, son. We are here to make the necessary arrangements for the cleaning and burial."

"I'd like to see my father first," Ashif says.

"His body has been moved to the funeral home," Naushad says.

"We needed to be speedy, you see," Shamshu Bhai adds. "We have to bury within forty-eight hours of death."

"I'd like to go to the funeral home, then." Ashif feels that everything is happening too quickly. Yet too slowly. As if a tornado is spinning around him in slow motion.

"Impossible, son," Shamshu Bhai says. "It is a private matter between Allah and the departed soul."

"Private matter!" Ashif says more loudly than he intended. "But I'm his son."

"They are from the Ghusal Committee, son," Layla says, clutching her purse. "Please, we must respect them."

"Ash," Arzeen says, handing him a paper cone. "Have some water."

"Please, let me explain," Naushad continues, gently touching Ashif's elbow. "In our *tariqa*, the body means nothing. Once the soul departs, it's just an empty vessel. There is no value in it."

The paper cone trembles in Ashif's hands.

"Come, sit down," Shamshu Bhai says, gently leading him to a chair.

Ashif sits down. The antiseptic smell invades his nostrils again, making his stomach churn. An image from his high school biology class forms in his mind: jars of frogs lining a shelf. Bodies suspended in formaldehyde. His father is not alive, not dead. All those hours, while Ashif was sleeping last night, during his run this morning, during his meetings. His father was dead. Why didn't he know earlier? He should have known earlier.

"Your father will not be alone," Shamshu Bhai says, shaking his head. "We will be with him, you see. We are the guardians of the body."

He knows the Ghusal Committee is here to help, but it feels as if they're vultures circling his father's body. "May I at least accompany you?" he asks, his voice breaking.

"No, son. I'm so sorry, but you can't," Shamshu Bhai replies.

"It's our job to ready him for his journey back home into the hands of Allah," Naushad says. "And that's a highly private and sacred ceremony." He then goes on to explain that the body will be cleansed at the funeral home according to Ismaili rites and rituals. After, holy water will be poured over his body, like a baptism, before he's shrouded in a simple white cloth so that he can be returned to the Almighty in the same state he arrived in. Dust to dust.

"I just want to see him," Ashif says desperately, opening and closing his fist, as if he's trying to grasp the light. "One last time. Please."

"You will have a chance to see him, I promise you. Twice, actually," Shamshu Bhai says, trying to reassure him.

"There will a private *chanta*–holy water ceremony before the funeral and again, during the *chele anjali*, the last viewing, at the funeral." He goes on to explain that the private *chanta* ceremony will be led by Mukhi Sahib and is only for immediate family. Each member, if they choose, will be able to perform the *chanta* ceremony. They will kneel over the coffin and ask Allah for forgiveness on behalf of the deceased. Mukhi Sahib will then spray the family member's face with holy water, a surrogate repentant. After the private ceremony, the funeral will be open to the public for the last viewing before the body is finally taken to the Ismaili graveyard.

Ashif feels numb. He won't be able recognize his father with his body cocooned in a white cloth like a pupa. He will only get to see part of his face. Nothing else. He looks up at the circular fluorescent lights mounted on the ceiling and tries to remember what his father looks like. But no images come to mind, as if the light has erased his father from memory. As if he'd never even existed.

At last, Ashif stands up, his legs still shaky under him. The hospital walls are closing in on him. His breath quickens, his heart races faster. He needs to get outside. He can't breathe.

"I have to go, Mummy," he tells Layla.

"Go where?" Layla asks, puzzled. She wraps her hands over her knees.

The seniors continue to rock back and forth in unison, praying silently.

"I don't know. I just need some fresh air," he says, struggling to explain.

"Turn on the fan," an old lady says to her husband, pointing at the ceiling. "The boy needs air."

"No, it's okay, Uncle," Ashif interjects. "I just need to be outside for a while."

"Maybe you can go later?" the man switches on the ceiling fan. "Now is the time for prayer."

The seniors nod in unison.

"Don't go, *dhikro*," a senior implores, dabbing her eyes with a handkerchief folded into a square. "Your mother needs you. It is her darkest hour."

"Paradise is at your mother's feet, son," adds another.

"Our prayers will help lift your father's soul to heaven. Like a spiritual wind, you see."

"And into *Fana Fillah*. 'To Him we belong and to Him shall we return.' It is his birthright as a Muslim. Submerge himself into the Almighty. Become one with Allah."

"Stay and pray with us. This is your duty."

Ashif looks from face to face until each one becomes the next, then the next. The room starts to revolve, at first slowly, then faster and faster until he can no longer focus. He sits down, his legs trembling.

"We mustn't delay matters any further," continues a senior, tilting his fedora hat up. "We were praying for his recovery, *kumbey*, the man had already expired. There's no time to waste."

"Yes, we've got to steer him back onto the right path, the path of *Siratal-Mustaqeem*. Allah is waiting."

Layla shoots up to standing. She is ferocious. Powerful. A tigress attacking a predator threatening her cub. "Then let Him wait!" she shouts. "Who are *you* to tell *my son* what to do?"

Ashif looks up. The seniors stare at Layla in disbelief. One elbows another. Others whisper. Someone yells, "*Pisha Mowla!* Such disrespect." One man leaves the room, shaking his head. Two women clap.

"He is *my* son and he will do as *he* wishes," she says then heads for the door. "Come, son," she says, and Ashif follows.

In the hallway, Layla reaches up and takes Ashif's face in her hands. "Go, son. Do what you need to do."

"Are you sure, Mummy?"

"Yes, I am sure."

"But will you be okay alone?"

"Of course, I will be fine. And I won't be alone. Where are they going to go," she asks, pointing a thumb over her shoulder, "with their *bhoffu*-broken legs?"

Ashif laughs. So does she. They kiss goodbye.

"I'll be back, Mummy."

"I know, *bheta*," she says and gives her son one final kiss.

Ashif walks briskly toward the exit, the heels of his shoes tap-tapping against the tile.

"Hey, Ash," a voice calls from behind him.

Ashif turns to see Arzeen following him down the long hall-way. He stops and walks toward her.

"I didn't want to give these to your mother." She hands him a set of forms. "The police report for the car accident. And the forms to release your father's car."

"Okay, thanks." He glances at the papers. At the top of the first page, the Queen's insignia with the words R.H. QUEEN REGINA underneath. A stamp diagonally across the page reads INVESTIGATION CLOSED.

"Also, this . . ." Arzeen removes an envelope from the front pocket of her scrubs. "Shafina sends her condolences."

"She's here?" He glances around, his heart pounding.

"No, she sent an email from New York." Arzeen hands him the envelope. "I printed it out for you."

"New York?" he asks, taking the envelope.

"Well, she's based in Cairo. She's a photojournalist for a start-up news organization called Aljazohra or something like that. I can never get it right."

Ashif can see Shafina in her Annie Lennox T-shirt, a short skirt, and army boots, walking the desert with a group of women in hijab, a massive camera around her neck. He laughs out loud.

"What's so funny?"

"Nothing," he says. "It's just impressive. But then, Shafina's always been impressive."

Arzeen furrows her brows as if she finds his response confusing. "We're so worried about her, but if we say anything to her she quotes people like Prince to us as if she's quoting the Imam's *firmans. Strong spirits transcend rules.* The girl's crazy is all I can tell you."

Shafina's words come rushing back to him. "We all find our own way to the divine. My religion just happens to be music and poetry."

"She's in New York right now covering that World Trade Center bombing trial. She's always putting herself in precarious situations," Arzeen says.

Ashif imagines Shafina with that massive volume of Rumi in hand, ready to thump any man who dares touch her.

"But Mom and Dad are hopeful, we all are, that she'll tire herself out and come back home. Settle down and have a normal life, you know? I mean, how long can you live like a nomad, right? She has to grow up sometime." Arzeen shakes her head disdainfully. "I have no idea what happened with you guys, Ash, but I don't blame you. No one does. We all know what a handful she is." Arzeen stops herself, takes his hand in hers.

"Sorry, Ash. You've got so much on your mind and here I am going on about nothing."

"No, it's okay. I can't tell you how happy I am to hear about Shafina. It's just that I need to go."

"Of course." She reaches up on her toes and kisses him goodbye. "Please call me or Al-Karim if you need anything, okay?"

"Okay, thanks. And thanks for this, too." He waves the envelope in the air, then tucks it into his jacket pocket.

A burst of cold air hits him as he steps through the hospital's revolving doors. He doesn't bother to button up his winter jacket or put on his gloves. He's relieved to be out of the hospital. It's not even noon and it feels as if it's the end of the day. He takes a deep breath and crosses the road to the empty taxi stand where he sets his briefcase down and reviews the police report. On the second page of the report is a map with an *X* where his father's car was found and another *X* where the body was located. The third page: a release form with the insurance company's details and a business card for the car compound.

A taxi with a mound of snow on the roof, like a square igloo, pulls up. Ashif jumps in.

The driver tilts the rearview mirror and looks at Ashif. "Where to?"

Chapter 20

WHEN MANSOOR WAKES, HIS head is pressed against the steering wheel. His body is slumped and stiff, as if he has been motionless for a long time. He lifts his head slowly and pats a palm to his head, expecting blood. But there isn't any. A CD tape whirs in its deck, Dolly's voice stuck on the same line of "Islands in the Stream." Moonlight pours into the car, refracting through the icy windshield.

Mansoor flicks on the windshield wipers. They rise hesitantly over the frost. He leans forward and peers outside, but he cannot see anything. He tries to open the driver's door, but it is stuck. He pushes his shoulder against it. Still nothing. He lifts himself off his seat and climbs into the passenger seat. A sharp pain runs down the length of his leg. He groans softly but continues. He props one arm on the steering wheel and twists himself out of the driver's seat. The passenger door beeps intermittently when he opens it.

He stumbles out, his feet sinking into snow. He is at the bottom of a ditch. The yellow cone of the car's headlights cut the dark like a diver's torch in a dark sea. The engine is still on, purring softly like a sleeping animal. He zips up his winter jacket and inspects the Impala. A mass of mangled steel and snow. An accident! He's been in an accident? With elephants? He was on his way from Kampala to Kisumu to meet Layla for the first time. Near Nairobi, close to the Great Rift Valley, he turned a sharp corner and nearly drove straight into a herd of elephants with a newborn calf. He was in a Range Rover, but it would not protect him from the wrath of an elephant mother. Nothing could. He quickly cranked the gearshift and drove his vehicle into a ditch. The herd passed but he was stuck, his tires knee-deep in mud. It took eight Maasai to push the Rover up and out of the ditch. That week, Neil Armstrong made a soft landing on the moon. When he recounted the story to Layla's family, he joked that he too had made a soft landing, but on mud—to which everyone laughed and clapped.

Not mud this time. Snow. He had never been in a car accident in Canada. Fender-benders, sure. A few nicks here and there. Nothing serious; nothing he had to report. These things happen. Especially when he was new in the country and still getting used to driving on the right and managing icy roads. But never an accident! He had always been so careful. There was that time when he was pulled over for driving under the influence. A police officer had stopped him when he saw Mansoor's car waver on Memorial Drive. This after a business dinner with a real estate agent who specialized in small businesses. The officer gave him a warning, then let him go. His generosity made Mansoor reconsider his habit. After all, in Kampala, men would drive themselves home after an evening of drinking whether it was City Bar, the casino, or a round of golf. He was so grateful for the kindness of that officer. In Uganda, he would have had to grease his palm. It only deepened his loyalty to Canada. Justice and fairness in all matters.

Mansoor hears a faint whir. An approaching car? He climbs out of the ditch, his body a reluctant helper. When he gets to the top, he stands on the shoulder and surveys the long, straight road, which is flanked on both sides by dark fields. The road is empty. He leans down to get a closer look at the ground. A pain throbs in his right temple, then disappears as quickly as it came. He touches his fingers to the asphalt in the same way he touched the tarmac when they first landed in Canada at Montreal-Dorval International Airport, a gesture of thanks and relief. The road is covered in a light snow, but otherwise it seems fine. No black ice. No drifts.

He must call for help. He slides back down into the ditch and retrieves his cellphone from the car. He dials 9-1-1. The word DIALING remains fixed on the screen. He lifts the phone to the sky like an offering, hoping to catch a signal. Still nothing. He climbs back up the ditch and tries again. No service.

He traces a circle, still holding the phone high. In the distance, an orange haze lights the night sky. The city! He can't be that far from home. He considers his options. He can wait here for a passing car. He checks his cellphone for the time. Almost midnight. Who's going to drive by at this hour, especially on a country road? He might wait all night. Or he can walk to a main road where the chance of getting help is better. More passing cars. Maybe a gas station or a store. Who knows, maybe he can even walk home. Can't be more than a few kilometres, maybe a little more. The night is not especially cold.

He shimmies back down the ditch to retrieve his things from the car. When he pulls open the front passenger door, Dolly's voice tumbles out of the car, rolling away over the fields into the dark. He leans into the car, his hurt leg jutting out like a plank, and tries to turn off the ignition. But the key is stuck. He pushes on the hazard lights. Just in case someone drives by.

He walks to the back of his Impala and snaps open the trunk. He leans in past the sandbags and retrieves a bag with the words EMERGENCY KIT scrawled across the front. Mansoor made the kit from an old boxy briefcase, one he used during those years when he spent his days off from Patterson to travel the province in search of a business.

He empties out the contents: booster cables, a flashlight that he snaps on and off to make sure it is working, seven feet of waterproof rope, flares, a medical kit, and a folded SOS sign that can be pressed against the inside of a windshield or else placed on the roof of the car. For a moment, he considers displaying the sign. But then laughs. As if anyone will see it. It's too dark. Besides, this isn't an emergency. No one is dying here.

Inside the case, there is also a medical kit. He snaps it open. Bandages, hydrogen peroxide, scissors, and a little bottle with a red rooster. His Wake-Ups pills. He keeps a bottle here in case he finishes the one in his briefcase. Only now does it occur to him that perhaps he fell asleep at the wheel. Is that how he ended up in this ditch? But he banishes the thought immediately. Impossible! He even had a cup of coffee after eating his dinner at Harry's Sports Bar. Or was it a whisky? He pauses. He's not sure. Doesn't matter! He was wide awake when he started his drive, of that much he is sure.

Mansoor turns away from his wrecked car and briefly surveys the landscape. The dark fields extend to the horizon and merge seamlessly with the night sky. A perfect circle. A barbed-wire fence separates the ditch from the field. This was one of the reasons he was drawn to Alberta. The sheer immensity of the land, the feeling that anything was possible here.

In Montreal, Mansoor was asked to choose the province his family wanted to live in. First, he studied the wall map of Canada pinned up at the immigration office. A massive country, longer than his outstretched arms. He developed catchy acronyms to remember key facts like BAS MOQ, which translated to "I've had enough." Each letter represented the large provinces, west to east: British Columbia, Alberta, Saskatchewan, Manitoba, Ontario, and Quebec. After grasping the basics of Canadian geography, he pored through the library at the immigration office. The collection included a few books of fiction. But what he really wanted was to understand the real Canada so he studied the non-fiction—travel books and history books—making a list of the beneficial features of each major city. He crossed off Montreal immediately. It reminded him too much of Vienna with its cobblestone roads, old buildings, and its stubborn insistence on tradition. He had no interest in holding on to the past. And who wanted to be a part of such an unwelcoming society? One that insisted on one language, one way of doing things? Not him. Not after Uganda. Toronto also seemed mired in the old with its mess of intertwining streets named after old battles, royal figures, and war heroes. Roncesvalles, Queen, King, Bathurst. Tied to the old country like a child to a mother's apron strings. Suffocating—all this history staring down at you at every turn. He ruled out Vancouver and the Maritime provinces. Vancouver with an ocean at the base of its mountains and St. John's with its craggy harbour. Too much beauty can lull a person into a false sense of well-being. It breeds laziness. Nobody works hard in coastal cities. They think they are on vacation all the time. It was business-minded Alberta, and Calgary, in particular, that appealed to him. A city clearly divided into quadrants, the streets and avenues numbered and easy to follow. If a street was named, it was for the neighbourhood, not for some bygone man, so that all the streets in Pineridge started with the letter P. That made complete sense. That's how every city should be designed. He also liked Alberta's landscape. Clear lines, straight roads, neatly cut hectares, perfect rolls of hay. Even the colours were simple: golden fields, blue skies, emerald lakes. But most of all, he felt a deep kinship with Alberta's history—the prairie homesteaders who worked relentlessly to break and settle the land through the harshest of winters and with hardly any tools or resources. They were strong. Resilient. Self-sufficient. Just like him. Just like his father. The Wild Wild West. A blank slate where he could make his mark.

"Why Alberta?" Lyle, the volunteer at the immigration office, asked when Mansoor told him his decision.

"My father was a cowboy, you see. And so am I."

Lyle laughed. "Right on, man. And here I thought you were Indian."

"Of course not!"

"You'll fit right in there, man," Lyle said, sliding his yellow tinted glasses up the ridge of his nose. He then scribbled on the immigration forms and handed them to him. "Congratulations, Mansoor. Canada welcomes you."

In the distance, he sees the faint outline of a structure. Moonlight reflects off the roof. He can't make it out clearly. A house or maybe a barn? Even if it is a barn, the farmhouse will be close by. Maybe he should walk there instead and ask the farmer to use his phone? It is closer than the main highway. Besides, he doesn't know which way to start walking. He scans the dark fields— there must be a road that leads to the house, but finding it may be hard. Cutting across the field is the most rational decision.

Mansoor steps one leg through the barbed-wire fence and checks the depth of snow like a swimmer testing the temperature of the water before diving in. He sinks down to his ankles. His galoshes will not do.

He returns to the trunk where he pulls out the pair of mukluks he keeps there for just such an occasion. He bought the boots—with matching ones for Ashif and for Layla, too—for their first winter in Canada. They were expensive, but he wanted his family to be warm. "Like moon boots, Pappa!" Ashif squealed when Mansoor gave them to him. "That's right. One small step for us, one giant step for mankind."

Mansoor had assumed they were the best model to buy. After all, the Inuit wore them. But it didn't take long for him to realize that they were the wrong boots for Calgary. Fine in Edmonton, Red Deer, Banff, or other parts of the country. But in Calgary, chinooks were the problem. Warm winds that blew in and turned streets of snow into pools of slush. The mukluks became waterlogged, making it difficult to walk. But they would do well for cutting across a field of snow. He sits down on the bumper and slips them on.

He is about to close the trunk when he decides to also take the boxy briefcase with him. He will look more respectable this way—a businessman, which he is of course. He does not want to startle the farmer. They have guns! They might think he is a traveling salesman—someone who wants to sell them a vacuum cleaner or solicit donations for a church. This thought makes Mansoor laugh. Well, better that than a wanderer. He would certainly never open his door to someone like that, especially if his family was at home. But then it occurs to him that a salesman is homeless; he is always on the road.

Mansoor slips his briefcase between the barbed wire fence. He ducks down and slides one leg in. He is about to pull his second leg through when his pants catch on the wire. He tugs the fabric free and rolls into the snowfield like a boxer into a ring. He stands up immediately; dusts the snow off. He reaches for his flashlight and inspects his leg. His pants are slightly torn and on his calf, a hairline cut. Nothing serious. There is no blood. Just a minor battle scar. He laughs and shakes his leg vigorously as if to rejuvenate it.

He glances back at the road and considers for moment if he should just wait for someone to drive by. He checks his watch: half-past midnight. He reviews the logic of his decision: too late for a passing car, short distance to the farmhouse, reasonable temperatures. Yes, this is a good idea. He flips the hood of his coat over his head and puts on his gloves. He begins his walk to the farmhouse, his sales bag swinging from one hand, his car's hazard lights blinking behind him.

Chapter 21

THE CAR COMPOUND IS located in an industrial park off Blackfoot Trail in the southeast quadrant of the city. Inside the garage, a man in greasy striped coveralls and a Calgary Flames toque flips through the forms. An oval patch over his chest reads BRANDON. "Accident or tow?" he asks.

"Accident." Ashif turns his gaze to the window. In the distance, he glimpses the huddle of the city's skyscrapers, like concrete mountains. A plane arcs over the skyline. Only yesterday he walked out of the business lounge at the airport, his stride quick and sure. He never said goodbye. He never turned around, not even for one last look. If only he'd taken one last look. All he remembers is his father's hand, the veins green and bulbous, pushing the envelope with his name on it back at Ashif.

Brandon leads Ashif outside to the yard of cars. They zigzag past what seems like hundreds of cars, the snow crunching under their feet. Some of the cars are unrecognizable, crumpled empty shells. Others are flattened into sheets of metal, piled one on top of the other. A few are buried, rounded bodies of snow and ice like frozen tombs.

"Here it is. Chevy Impala. They're good cars. If you like American, that is."

His father's words run through his head. When you weigh the pros and cons, Impala always comes out on top.

Ashif surveys the car. The front right side of the car is damaged, a large indent, like a crater, on the body. The hood on that side is squeezed up, a steel wave frozen in place.

"Doesn't look too bad to me," Brandon says. "Chances are we can have it back to you in no time."

"Can I have my father back, too?" Ashif wants to say.

Ashif squats down, the edge of his winter coat gathering on the snow, and inspects the damage from close range. He pulls at the fingertips of one glove to remove it, and is about to touch the damaged quarter panel when Brandon stops him.

"Please don't touch anything. The insurance folks need to see it first."

"Okay."

A long steady bell rings. Brandon gazes back at the garage. "Got another customer. I'll be right back."

When Brandon's out of sight, Ashif sweeps a gloved hand over a window to clear the snow and peers in. He can't see anything through the frost. He tests the driver's side door. It's locked. He tries the back door. To his surprise, it opens. He glances back at the garage then throws his briefcase in and slides inside.

Light seeps through the frosty windows, casting a pale glow over the interior, like light seeping through cracks of ice. The shadow of a pine-tree air freshener hangs from the rear-view mirror. He sees his father's head, too. A circle like a full moon that almost touches the roof. He reaches out to touch it.

Ashif feels something under his feet. He reaches up for the light switch but it doesn't work. He clicks on his cellphone and pans the lighted screen over the interior. The floor and seat are littered with debris, which surprises him. His father's car was always so well-organized and tidy. Something shimmers between the front seats. A dry-cleaning sheath. He rubs his fingers against the edge of the sheath to separate the plastic, then knots it at one end.

He scoops up paper cups, a crushed water bottle, a yellow chamois cloth. From under a seat, a box of tissues patterned with wild geese. He yanks the pine-tree air freshener off the rear-view mirror, presses it to his nose before throwing it into the bag. Then he reaches deep into the front seat and retrieves the garbage from the floor: gum wrappers, an empty can of club soda, crumpled-up serviettes. He pushes his feet against the back seat to steady himself and stretches to the driver's door. In the side panel, he finds several maps neatly banded together with elastic, one of Canada, the others of Alberta, as well as several pens. He tears the suede sleeve from the steering wheel, his fingers fumbling with the strings. Then he shifts to the other side, snaps open the glove compartment, and continues his excavation. He finds a vinyl organizer and a black notebook with a pen clipped to the coil binding. He throws them into the thin, sagging bag. From the front seat, he clatters together the handful of CDs. His breath is shallow, his brow wet. He pats the pockets on the back of the front seats as if he is frisking them. He reaches in and removes handfuls of small notebooks, bundled into sets of four.

Suddenly, the front passenger door jerks open. Sunshine pours in. Ashif shields his eyes.

Brandon leans into the car, blocking the light. "Hey! What are you doing in there?"

"I'm leaving," Ashif says, shoving the notebooks into the bag.

"Just put the stuff back in the car and I'll pretend it never happened, okay?" Brandon offers.

"I'm taking it," he says, the bag firmly in his grip.

"Fine. Do what you want." Brandon slams the back door shut. "But you can kiss your insurance goodbye. They'll probably scrap the car."

Ashif stops and faces Brandon. "Let them! He's dead. He's dead," he says like a mantra as if he's trying to convince himself that it's true.

Ashif walks to the service road at the entrance of the compound. His legs feel heavy yet weak, like steel columns wobbling. He sets down his briefcase and the dry-cleaning bag on a clear patch of road and waits to flag down a taxi. It takes him a few minutes to remember that it's impossible to flag down a taxi in Calgary. You have to call for one. He reaches for his cell, but the phone is dead. Using it as a flashlight must have drained the battery. He picks up his briefcase and heaves the bag over his shoulder, a hobo in a business suit. He crosses the road to the car rental shop, "M.G. Visram & Son Dry Cleaners, Ltd: Suiting Canada Since 1987" bobbing against his back.

The young woman is efficient. Within ten minutes, he's back outside, unplugging the rental from the electrical post. The car is mid-sized, much smaller than his father's Chevy Impala, but bigger than any car he would buy, not that he's ever owned one. It's been years since he's driven—he's only kept up his driver's licence to use as ID.

He slips off his jacket and is about to throw it in the back seat when the letter from Shafina falls out. He picks it up and dusts the snow off. He then steps into the driver's seat, surprised by the new-car smell. He tucks the letter into a corner of the dash. He wraps his fingers around the steering wheel. It feels good in his hands. He twists the wheel one way then the other, like a child pretending to drive.

He must have been six, no older. He was standing on the sofa on the second floor of their apartment building with his face pressed to the glass, watching, as always, for his father to come home from his job at Patterson Used Cars & Trucks. He watched as one bus after the other passed. Then there he was, stepping out of a long blue automobile.

"Mummy!" Ashif screamed. "Pappa's home. With a car!"

His father saw him in the window and waved him down.

Ashif pulled on his mukluks, even though it was a warm chinook day and the streets were dotted with pools of melting snow. "Let's go, Mummy!"

Outside, Layla took his hand in hers to cross the street, but he dropped it as soon as he could and ran to his father. Mansoor crouched down with open arms and lifted his son up. He tried to wrap his small hands around his father's forearm, but he couldn't. They were so big.

Mansoor slapped the roof of the car. "So, what do you think?" he asked. "Chevy Impala."

"Very nice!" Layla said.

"Only a matter of time before I turn this into a brand-new Lincoln Continental. We'll dress up and go to the best restaurant. How's that, Layla?"

Layla nodded and laughed.

Ashif imagined his father in a black tuxedo, shouting "Abracadabra-Alakazam!" as he turned this car into another, then another, and another.

Mansoor kneeled down to Ashif. "And you? What's your expert opinion, sir?"

"Super-duper."

Mansoor rustled his hair. "Let's go for a drive. Come, Layla, all of us."

"You go ahead. I still haven't finished cooking," Layla said.

"Okay. It'll be just the men today," Mansoor said, turning to Ashif. "Ready, son?"

"Yes!" Ashif said then hesitated. He didn't want to get his mukluks wet. "My boots, Pappa."

Mansoor scooped him back up and carried him to the passenger side. In his father's arms, he soared over the slushy pools, like an astronaut over the moon's craters.

"Wear your seat belt," Layla called after them.

His father swung open the door and sat Ashif inside.

Mansoor stepped into the driver's side and patted the dashboard. "There are two kinds of people in the world, son. Those who ride buses and those who drive cars. And what kind are we?"

"Car people!"

"Look, it has all the latest gadgets: cruise control, double tape deck instead of an eight-track, 140 horsepower—a muscle car!" Mansoor said, turning the ignition. The car roared to life. The dashboard lit up, a halo of green under the wood panelling.

"Just like a spaceship, Pappa!"

"Our mission: to go where no man has gone before."

Mansoor drove them up and down the flat, well-organized streets of Calgary. Near Bowness Park, they came to a hill. They climbed up and zoomed down many times, with Mansoor's hands floating above the steering wheel and Ashif's in the air, screaming with the thrill of it.

On their way home, Mansoor pulled the car into an empty parking lot. "Son, your turn now."

Ashif giggled with nervous excitement. "But I'm too small."

"Don't worry. I'll be right here."

He sat on his father's lap, his back pressed against his father's chest. The sweet-spice smell of Yardley's hair cream filled his nostrils. He could barely see over the dashboard, the street a black slither. His father lifted his hands to the steering wheel and laid his own hands on top.

"Ready, Captain Visram?" Mansoor asked, shifting the car into drive.

Ashif nodded.

"Are you super-duper sure, Captain?"

Ashif laughed and gave him a thumbs-up.

First, they drove in circles around the parking lot. He was amazed at how a small turn of the wheel could turn so much steel. They were driving down a street where all the houses looked like castles when suddenly a golden dog leapt into the road in front of them. The car screeched to a halt. Ashif's head hit the steering wheel and snapped back. He started to cry, mostly from the shock and partly from the pain. Mansoor quickly pulled the car over and set his son back into the passenger side.

"Let's see," he said, pushing Ashif's curls off his forehead. "It's hardly anything. You'll be fine, son."

Ashif tried to hold back his tears, but he couldn't; they came pouring down his cheeks.

"Boys don't cry, do they?"

Ashif shook his head. He wiped his tears away with broad, clumsy strokes.

"Come on, show me your muscles."

Ashif flexed his arms for his father.

Mansoor squeezed his biceps. "Pretty good. Soon, you'll be strong as me."

Ashif basked in the warm glow of his father's praise.

Ashif turns the key in the ignition and the rental car starts to purr. The dry-cleaning bag stuffed with the gleanings from his father's car sits slumped on the passenger seat. He roots through it for the black notebooks, bundled together in fours. It surprises him that his father kept a journal. He yanks off an elastic band, eager to see what his father had written.

He opens one with the title A-M-J 1996 on the cover. The first page is divided into four columns: DATE, START, END, KMS. At the bottom, a total for the kilometres driven. On the next page, the total carries forward and the counting starts again. He throws the book down, picks up another, shuffling through the pages for a note, a few words. Then another. And another. Not even one sentence. Only a log of all the kilometres he'd driven to and from the dry cleaners, to and from the gas station. Numbers. Nothing but numbers. Deflated, he tosses them into the back, where they scatter across the seat and the floor.

He reaches again into the dry-cleaning bag and pulls out the suede steering-wheel cover and the police report. He fits the suede cover over the steering wheel, manoeuvring his hands through the wheel to tighten its strings. The wheel now feels soft and strong under his hands. He unfolds the map attached to the police report, traces the distance between the two *X*s with a finger. From where the car was found and where his father's body was found. Not even a kilometre.

What happened in such a short distance, Pappa? Where were you trying to get to?

Ashif had only been a few kilometres away in his airport hotel room. His day had been like the day before. A long day of meetings followed by a quick dinner with Mel. After, he lay in his hotel bed and mindlessly flipped through the TV channels. He emptied the bar fridge, too. He wanted to forget his day, as he always did. Escape his body. His life. Meanwhile, his father was in a farm field, fighting for his. Ashif's heart suddenly feels hollow, as if it's pumping air, not blood. He backs the car out of its parking spot and begins his journey.

On McKnight Boulevard, he has a full view of the Rockies, a canvas of snow and rock against the blue sky. He feels a magnetic pull toward the mountains, as if there's a compass inside his body guiding him. He had intended to drive north to Airdrie, but suddenly the vastness of the prairies makes him feel as though he's adrift in an ocean. He remembers this feeling even as a child. There was no easy way to locate yourself in such a landscape. No markers, no reference points, just wide-open space, a feeling that you could easily disappear.

The mountains will ground him, he thinks. Root him somehow.

At Deerfoot Trail, he turns south then exits westbound onto the Trans-Canada Highway, a single road laid across the country, connecting the Atlantic and Pacific Oceans, like an artery across a massive body. Behind him, the city recedes and ahead, the fields of snow spread themselves open on either side. The mountains are still hundreds of kilometres away, but he feels as though he could reach out and touch them from here.

He keeps his eyes focused on the solid white line that divides the highway in two. Soon, speed turns to stillness. He feels as if he isn't moving at all, as if he's suspended in the landscape. He reaches into the dry-cleaning bag and his hand falls on a CD. He lifts it out and glances at the cover. *Kenny Rogers & Dolly Parton, Greatest Hits.* He rubs the disc on his chest, slips it into the stereo's socket, and presses play.

Chapter 22

MANSOOR HEARS THE CRACK first. Like a gunshot that ricochets across the open field. The back of his foot plunges down. His body falls backward and then straight down as if the earth opened its jaws and swallowed him whole. He flails his arms frantically, gasping, instinctively trying to hold his briefcase out of the water as if it were filled with valuable documents instead of useless items. Ice crackles and breaks. His clothes balloon with water. When he touches the bottom of the pond, he tries to stand up and steady himself. His feet slide on rocks. He slips and falls several times. When he finally stands up, he is waist-deep in icy water. He pushes through the slush, portaging his briefcase above him like a canoe. He finds his way to the edge of the pond. He crawls out. He beaches himself on the snow and tries to catch his breath.

As he lies there, an airplane arcs across the sky like a firefly across a dark field. For a moment, this shift in perspective gives him immense pleasure. A large machine made so small. But then it occurs to him that he too has been reduced. He is just a dot in this darkness. How easy it would be to disappear. He quickly replaces these thoughts with facts. An airplane is massive. It weighs several tonnes, yet it flies, carries hundreds of passengers, circumnavigates the earth thousands of times. A tireless explorer.

Mansoor stands up. His legs feel heavy. His clothes and mukluks have begun to freeze. He turns back to the road. The car's hazard lights still blink in the distance. Should he return to the car? Or continue to the farmhouse? They are equidistant apart from here, he thinks, though he cannot be sure. But the chances of someone driving by at this hour, he reminds himself, are slim. He picks up his briefcase and continues toward the farmhouse.

A few minutes later, his breath turns shallow and he begins to shiver. His briefcase slips from his hand into the snow. "Leave it, Visram. You can come back and get it in the morning when it's light out. . . . No, take it now." He bends down to pick it up, but stumbles. He falls to his knees. He pushes up and starts again. "Just a little longer," he tells himself, willing his body to cooperate. He keeps his gaze on the farmhouse and marches forward.

Soon, his clothes become as hard as armour. He laughs. He is a knight! "Faster!" he commands his legs. But they refuse. Each step is slower, more arduous, as if he's climbing Kilimanjaro. He is exhausted. The weight of his clothes pulls him down. He lies down for a moment to catch his breath. Above him, a roof of twinkling stars, and as he watches them, his thoughts begin to dim. "Stay awake!" he orders himself. But soon, he falls into a frozen slumber.

Mansoor picked up the fallen piece of paper from the floor and slid it across the dining table to Layla.

"Twenty-four hours?" she asked, examining the sketch for the new sign. VISRAM SPEEDY GAS & CONVENIENCE: OPEN 24 HOURS.

"I'm going to move into the station, but only until I can hire someone for the night shift." He drummed his fingers on the table. "It's the only way to improve sales."

The gas station was one of the only stops on the lonely stretch of highway between Rocky Mountain House and Red Deer, and until last year, it attracted a constant flow of customers. But now, hours went by without a single customer. The economy slipped into a deep recession and interest rates skyrocketed to close to twenty percent. In a matter of months, oil rigs were shut down and construction companies abandoned their sites, leaving behind communities of partially built structures like skeletons throughout the province. For several months now, Mansoor had been unable to make his loan payments on time and the bank had put him on notice.

"No." Layla shook her head. "I won't let you leave us. Not again. Sell that business. Please." She pushed the sheet back to him and crossed her arms. "I won't raise our children alone." Layla was three months pregnant.

"And who's going to buy it in this economy, Layla? Who?" He crumpled the drawing and threw it on the floor.

She turned away.

They sat in silence, then he pulled his chair close to her. "Look, Layla, I'm doing this for us. For the children. This is no way for us to be living." He tilted his head toward the window overlooking the townhouse parking lot.

"We have to make the sacrifice now. There's no other way." He took her hand in his. "How else are we going to make it in this country?"

She turned to him. "We will come with you."

"But I don't want you to be in the middle of nowhere. Not now. Not with the baby coming."

She had no argument to that. He also did not want to disrupt Ashif's education.

"It's just a temporary matter," he said.

"Promise me you'll be back by the time the baby is here."

"I promise."

Later that morning, they packed his things and he gave her a set of post-dated cheques.

Ashif stood on the sidewalk as Mansoor pulled his Chevy out of the driveway.

"Bye, Pappa." His hands were tucked into his jacket, his voice sheepish.

Mansoor parked the car and stepped out. He knelt down on one knee and held his son by his shoulders. "Remember what we talked about?"

"Yes." Ashif's eyes filled with tears.

It was the last thing Mansoor wanted, too. He'd already missed a year of his son's life and he didn't want to miss any more. But what choice did he have? He had to do it for the sake of the family. Taking care of the business was taking care of the family. He wiped his thumbs under his son's eyes. "You're eleven now, son. You're practically a man!" He gently punched him on the sides of his torso.

Ashif put his elbows up in feign defence. "I am?"

Mansoor tousled his son's curls. "Yes, you are. And when I'm not at home, guess who's the man of the house?"

"Me?" Ashif asked, tentatively.

"Exactly. That means you have to take care of Mummy for me, okay?"

"Okay."

"And soon, you'll have a baby brother or sister to help take care of, too."

Ashif was smiling.

That afternoon, Mansoor turned the office at the back of the gas station into his makeshift home. Other than his desk and filing cabinets, he didn't need much. A cot, a bar fridge, a small freezer, a microwave, a bar with a few bottles of whisky. He nailed hooks into the bathroom wall to hang his clothes; cardboard boxes served as a dresser. In front of the full-length mirror beside his desk, a set of free weights and a skipping rope.

Mansoor opened the lid of a small cooler. Inside, Layla had neatly stacked Tupperware containers, each one labelled with masking tape. Enough to last until his next visit. He removed two containers. One labelled chicken saag and the other one rice. He dumped the contents into a bowl then into the microwave. He picked up a set of dumbbells for biceps curls. The oven buzzed. He set the weights down. He took the bowl to his desk and sat down to work. It was five o'clock, but the winter sun had long since set. The store lights were on. The office was dark except for his desk lamp. Outside, the twenty-four-hour neon sign pulsed in the night sky.

A distant voice rolls across the dark fields, nudging Mansoor awake. He lifts his head gingerly and scans the fields. Nothing. Only the car's hazard lights blinking in the dark. He strains to hear a distant sound. Dolly?

His head drops back to the cushion of snow. He begins shivering again. He turns on his side and pushes himself back up to standing. The farmhouse. He has to get to the farmhouse. He tries to wiggle his toes, but he cannot feel them. The numbness hurts. He wishes he could shake them loose like ice cubes from a tray. He feels as if the signals from his brain to his body are being disconnected, snuffed out one by one. This only makes him want to try harder. He refocuses his mind and pushes the signals from his brain to his extremities. Go! Move! Do it! His legs jerk like an engine sputtering. But almost at once, they stall and buckle under him. He falls down. He tries to lift himself up again. But his limbs are heavy. His eyes are heavy. His brain begins to dim again. He reaches for his briefcase. He wants the SOS placard. But he can't pull the briefcase to him. He calls for help instead. "Hello," he mumbles to the fields. "Please help me. I am here. I am Mansoor Visram," he whispers, his voice trailing into the emptiness.

"My name means everything to me. I will not spoil it," Mansoor said to Gordon Ludlum, who sat across from him at the offices of Stanley, Ludlum, and Partners, Accountants & Receivers. The accountant's desk was awash with files and paper. Photographs of his family pocked the wall behind him.

"I know we've negotiated a good deal here, Mr. Visram. Forty percent of the original debt." Ludlum tapped a set of forms with the blunt edge of his pen. "But it might be easier, don't you think, to claim bankruptcy? Wipe the debt off the books instead of carrying it forward?"

"I prefer a receivership."

"It's very common right now, Mr. Visram. There's no shame in it at all. Everyone's doing it given the state of the economy and all."

Mansoor stood his ground.

Ludlum swivelled his leather chair from side to side like a hyena surveying a savannah. "You'd get your name back in seven years. The time will go by just like this." He snapped his fingers. "Lickity-split. You can open up another business then."

"No, I can't wait," Mansoor said, unable to keep the irritation from his voice. Nineteen-ninety-three felt like a lifetime away. "My decision is firm. Please, let's finish the necessary paperwork. I have a lot of other things to still do."

"Alrighty, Mr. Visram. As you wish." Ludlum pulled himself back to his desk. He scribbled in the date, August 26, 1986, on the duplicate set of forms, then placed them in front of Mansoor. "Right here, Mr. Visram," he said, tapping the pen to the signature line. "Your John Hancock, please."

That afternoon, Ludlum stood guard at the front door as Mansoor packed his car. A box of kitchen items, the fold-away cot, a suitcase. Nothing else. Not one office pen. Not one file. Everything now belonged to the bank. Behind him, the windows of the gas station were dull with brown paper. The gas pumps had been fitted with gunny sacks like morgue bags. The door was chained and locked, a Notice of Receivership nailed to the front. As Mansoor shifted into drive, his mind flashed back to Uganda. The army officers storming into his store with machetes. Mansoor quietly walking out of Visram P. Govindji & Son. "All the best to you, Mr. Visram," Ludlum called out over the crunch of gravel as Mansoor drove away.

Mansoor wakes to a fluting sound, a distant melody like a muezzin's call. He half-opens his eyes. Dark fields extend to the horizon and merge seamlessly with the night sky. A perfect circle. The prairie hills are massive frozen waves. He feels something pecking at his feet. He lifts his head. A small domed shape bobs up and down at his feet, hammering at his icy body. The bird flies up and hovers over his chest. Her body is brilliant blue; her crown golden. Her breast is plump and glazed with rhinestone tassels instead of feathers. Mansoor is amazed that she can fly. He swipes the air and tries to catch her, but she flies up and out of reach. He plants his hands on the snow and struggles to stand, his veins a map of frozen rivers. The bird flies ahead of him and waits, like a siren willing him forward. A few steps and he falls to his knees. His clothes are an armour of ice. In the distance, the city lights are a pale smudge in the sky. He tries to stand again but his body jars, a ship caught in icy waters. "Get up, Visram!" he orders himself. "Move!" Instead he falls, curls in the soft snow, and drifts off again. The bird lands on his shoulder. She nudges her way up to his ear and begins to sing.

Mansoor sat at the kitchen table with a cup of tea and the classified section of the *Calgary Herald* spread in front of him, searching the "Businesses for Sale" columns. With the recession, everyone was afraid to invest. They were at home nursing their wounds. Not him. He'd picked himself up. Reminded himself of what he needed to achieve. He would never give up. So he hatched a new plan. With the high number of bankruptcies and receiverships, many businesses would now sell well under market value. The law of supply and demand was in his favour and he would take advantage of it. In his negotiations with Ludlum, he had secured a line of credit. "For family expenses," he told Ludlum. "Until I can get back on my feet." But his plan was to tighten the household budget and use most of the money to start his new business. No bank would give him a loan so soon after his receivership. Now, he just needed to find something that required low capital investment. That was key.

"Anything good today?" Layla asked, setting a jar of jam and a stick of butter on the table before sitting down.

"Only a matter of time." He circled a video rental store and starred it.

"You want more?" she asked, pouring herself a cup of tea.

He shook his head. He reached for the butter stick and examined the label. On the front: a Dutch girl with blonde pigtails and the words *crème de la crème*. "Switch to the generic brand," he said.

"I tried it. It's no good." She reached for the butter knife.

"Try it again. We need to be more careful right now."

She set the knife down. "Okay."

On TV, the image behind the news anchorman was of the newly elected Prime Minister, Brian Mulroney. Mansoor had been torn on who to vote for in the election. In the end, he decided on Trudeau even as so many blamed him for the downfall of the economy. His loyalty couldn't be so easily snuffed out. If the baby had been a boy, he would have named him Pierre.

"What about Patterson?" Layla asks.

"What about him?" he asks, his gaze fixed on his newspaper.

"He liked you so much. Why not ask him for a job?"

It was bad enough working for Patterson, but now Patel ran the dealership. He'd seen his name fitted over the old sign. "I'd rather die than work for anyone again. Especially those fools."

"He would hire you straight away, I'm sure of it," she said, biting into the toast. "Then we wouldn't have to worry so much."

"Who said there was anything to worry about, Layla? I've got everything under control." He tapped his pen on the newspaper, creating a constellation of red dots. Why was she doubting him when what he needed more than ever was her unflinching support?

"I was only saying. A job might be easier than the hassle-bassle of business. You won't have to work so hard. And for so little."

The constellation of spots began to bleed into a mass of red. "This is only temporary. Once I find a new business, everything will go back to normal."

"Remember how they gave you paid vacation? Then we can go somewhere together. That would be so nice, no? Ashif would enjoy that. We all would."

Layla's words seared through him. What was she saying?

That he wasn't providing for the family? That he wasn't taking care of them? His anger, thick and murky before, distilled into one point: Layla. In his mind's eye, her face became Ludlum standing guard at the gas station, Patel's name on the dealership sign, Patterson lording over him all those years, the army officer pressing a machete to his neck. Her threw his chair back and stood up.

His arm shot out. Then again. He only stopped when he saw another face: his son standing at the kitchen door, watching him. From Ashif, he turned to see Layla, as if for the first time. She was huddled on the ground, her hands shielding her face.

Mansoor reached down for her. "Come ... I don't know ..."

She shuddered, weeping. "Go back inside your room," she called to Ashif. "Shut the door."

Instead of obeying his mother, Ashif rushed to her side. Mansoor cast his eyes away from his son's glare.

"Go now," she begged Ashif.

Ashif refused. He helped her up and pulled her away from his father.

Mansoor stood aside. He wanted to hide his face in shame.

Ashif led his mother to his room and shut the door behind them.

Mansoor's legs shook, as if an underground tremor was cracking his house in two. He ran out and drove away.

Mansoor wakes, shivering uncontrollably. "I'm sorry, Layla," he whimpers. "I'm so sorry." But there is no answer from his wife, only the silence of fields. He hears snow crunching under the weight of footsteps. He turns to see his son in a snowsuit and mukluks running to him with open arms. His heart lifts. "My boy!" But as Ashif gets closer, he's no longer a child but a young man, and Mansoor doesn't recognize him. His son like a stranger to him. Ashif stares down at him for a few moments, then walks away.

Mansoor's underarms are damp; the creases of his thighs soaked. He can feel pools of sweat under his clothes, like sweating while shovelling a sidewalk, the effort concealed underneath heavy clothing. The heat incongruous with the cold. The same dampness now grips his body. He tugs at the buttons on his jacket with his swollen fingers, frozen icicles. Dolly-bird falls out of the darkness again. She lands on his chest, pecks at his icy clothes. He begins to hum to stay awake. Instead, it puts him to sleep like a lullaby.

He circled the city for what seemed like hours, the soft purring of the engine soothing him. It was late but he didn't want to go home and face his family. He considered checking into a motel, but he didn't want to spend the money. He turned into an empty shopping plaza. He wondered if his family would worry about him if he did not come home. He hoped so, but he guessed they were probably relieved to have him gone. This thought hurt him deeply. But he couldn't blame them. Or maybe he could. Why did Layla provoke him? He fixed his brain on this idea and it eased his pain. His fists throbbed. One knuckle still bleeding. He pumped his hands open and closed, but it offered no relief. He wrapped his cut hand with a handkerchief, like medical gauze, then pushed his seat back and tried to rest.

The rising sun woke him in the morning, his vinyl jacket over him like a blanket, an empty bottle of whisky between his thighs. The sight of dried blood on the handkerchief stirred his shame. He pushed the memories of last night down.

He squinted against the brightness and pulled his seat upright. The shopping plaza parking lot was still empty. His was the only car. He threw the empty bottle onto the floor and stepped out. The air was cool and crisp. The sky robin's egg blue. He scanned the L-shaped plaza. Many of the storefronts were plastered with For Rent or For Lease signs. One had a bankruptcy sign, another read GOING OUT OF BUSINESS SALE! He rubbed his face and patted down his hair, then strolled up to the stores for a closer look.

One space, in particular, caught his attention. A closet-sized space. The sign on the door: IMPERIAL BANK OF ALBERTA. FULL-SERVICE BRANCH: NEW LOCATION! Underneath, a map of the plaza with the northwest corner highlighted. Next to the map, another sign: FOR LEASE. BARGAIN BASEMENT PRICES! An agent's name and phone number followed. Mansoor pressed his face to the window. Inside were two large cavities where the automated teller machines used to be. But what kind of business could you run from such a small space?

The towering plaza sign read CANYON CREEK PROFESSIONAL PLAZA. Somehow, he had made it to the other side of town. Canyon Creek was a good neighbourhood and bordered several truly affluent neighbourhoods: Bearspaw with its mansions, Pump Hill with its perfect vistas of the city, and Fish Creek with back doors that opened onto a golf course. Just then, a mint-green Mercedes pulled into the plaza and parked in front of the new bank site. Two men stepped out. Both were sharply dressed in suits. One of them unlocked the front door and they both disappeared inside. Bankers! It didn't matter if the economy was tough for everyone else, they, like all well-to-do types, had money pouring out of their pockets. That's when the idea came to him. Suits! These people wear suits. Suits need to be cleaned. They need to be tailored. A plan fell into place in his head easily and quickly, like beads in an abacus.

The small space was perfect for a dry-cleaning kiosk. A well-to-do neighbourhood was ideal. The store would serve only as a point of sale, a convenient place for people to drop off and pick up. He would farm the cleaning out to a plant, which would mean low overhead. No capital investment. That's it! All he needed was a counter (he would build that himself), a cash register (a used one would be fine), office supplies (he'd managed to take some from the gas station). The rent, he guessed, would be cheap. He couldn't imagine anyone else would want it. He would have to learn about the dry-cleaning business, but that wouldn't be a problem. How many other businesses had he become an expert in already? Business ran in his blood. Elated, he took out his pen and wrote the agent's phone number on his palm, then ran back the car.

Inside the car, his mind drilled down on the idea, working out the numbers. He could use the line of credit for this business, but then the family budget would be too tight. Layla made sure to remind him of that. He racked his brain for a solution. A second income! But not Ashif. He didn't want him to take on the responsibility of finances at such a young age. He needed to focus on his education. He decided to ask Layla to take a job instead. In Uganda, he would have never allowed it. A wife working would have been a sign of his failure as a husband. But he'd swallow his pride. Change with the times. He was, after all, a modern man. Besides, it was just temporary. Only until his business was on solid ground.

But what job could Layla take? He needed to think of a job that suited her, but one that wouldn't interfere with her duties at home. A home-based cooking business. Yes, that was it. She loved to cook. She would be able to take care of the family and earn some money, too. A perfect combination. That was what every woman wanted nowadays, and it gave him great pleasure to give her that, to help bring her into the modern age. The extra income would also allow them to keep some luxuries in their budget. Movies, outings to restaurants, day trips. Maybe even a vacation to Disneyland! That was what Layla wanted and he wanted that, too. There was nothing he wanted more than to give his family the life they used to have.

The closer he drove to his home, the further he felt from yesterday's event so that by the time he parked in front of his house, the details had faded away in his mind. When he saw Layla's bruised face, he dismissed her injuries, cordoned them off to the far recesses of his mind. He had nothing to do with that. He refused to make the connection that it was his hands, these hands, that did that to her. If for a moment the idea surfaced, his mind quickly reorganized the events and created a new story. She shouldn't have pushed him to the edge. She shouldn't have questioned him. It was her fault.

He never noticed the changes in his family. How Layla now tiptoed around him, how easily she cooperated with his every decision. He never noticed Ashif distancing himself from him, either. He just assumed he was busy with school. Mansoor had been away for over three years, yet Ashif had not lost his way. That was, for him, a testament of the solid foundation he had laid for him when he was younger. Recently, he'd even noticed him toting around books papered with the letters *B.S.* "What does it stand for?" he asked. "Business School," Ashif said, and Mansoor beamed with pride.

When Mansoor wakes, the pool of snow and ice under him is softer and deeper. His jacket is undone, his toque and gloves pulled off. He is boiling hot. With great effort, he rolls himself out of the wetness.

His father, tall and broad, looms over him. The top of his head grazes the sky, the moon like a giant spotlight behind him.

"Get up, boy!" he says, poking Mansoor with his silver-tipped cane. "This is not the finish line, boy!" He points his cane toward the farmhouse. "That way!"

"Water, Pappa," Mansoor whimpers. His mouth is parched; his tongue, thick and dry. He tries to swallow, but can't.

Govindji pokes at Mansoor again. "Get up, I said." He then turns and walks toward the farmhouse. "You've got to cross the finish line. It doesn't count if you don't."

Mansoor struggles to his feet. "Wait, Pappa! Let me show you . . ." He grabs at his pocket, but his fingers are thick icicles and he can't bend them.

Govindji turns back. In his hand, his gold pocket watch. "Hurry up, boy. I don't have all day."

Mansoor grasps the fax letter from Abrahams & Abrahams. "Look, Pappa! I got the money." He stumbles toward his father. He starts out upright but every few steps, he hunches over, further and further, the land softening under him. Soon, he is on all fours.

"What the hell are you? A monkey?" Govindji's voice booms through the darkness. "Stand up straight, boy! Progress means you must keep marching forward."

"I did it, Pappa! I'm going to get my plant," Mansoor cries. Above him the stars turn into twinkling store signs. His name lights up the sky. M.G. Visram & Son Dry Cleaners, Ltd., Suiting Canada Since 1987.

Govindji flips open the pocket watch. "Time's running out, boy."

"Look! You see there." Mansoor points to the sky. "That's where my plant is going." It was the reason he drove out here. To look at the property again. He holds out the fax letter to his father. "The digital revolution, Pappa. It's a goldmine. And we are going to be part of it!" He holds out the fax to his father. "I did it, Pappa! Just like I said I would!"

"Utter waste of my time!" Govindji flips his pocket watch closed. "Hard to believe you are my flesh and blood."

"No, Pappa. Don't say that."

"I knew you'd ruin everything. Turn everything to dust." He turns and fades into the darkness.

"Wait, Pappa..." Mansoor falls into the wet snow. A sudden gust whips the fax out of his hand and twirls it away.

Dolly-bird sweeps back and forth over Mansoor as if she is waving incense over his body. The fluting sound gets louder and louder. The land continues to soften and soon he is knee-deep in water. He hears a crashing sound. He turns to see the prairie hills collapsing in the distance like ice cliffs into an ocean. Chunks of land break off under his feet. The walls of the farmhouse slap open into the water. The slats float away with the other debris. A wasteland.

Water pools in circles around him. He loses his footing and falls, now fully immersed in water. He frantically searches for land, but there is none. The fields are an ocean. He thrashes his arms and legs, stretching his feet down, trying to touch the bottom. But he can't. Exhausted from the exertion, he hangs his head back and tries to rest. Waves wash over him. He coughs and sputters. His clothes melt off him like ice cubes in punch. Dolly-bird whirs above him, her wings pumping into a blur. Another Dolly-bird pops out from the blur, then another and another, until the sky is filled with birds. They chant in unison, their small faces like a congregation of old people. The beating of their wings stirs a gentle wind that ripples over the water and carries him forward. *Ya Rahman, Ya Rahim. The Most Compassionate, the Most Merciful.*

He lifts his head up. In the distance, a dark shape swishes effortlessly toward him. He flails his arms, splashing ice and water. "Help me, Pappa! Please . . ." A wave rolls in and sinks him into darkness.

When he emerges, a woman reaches down from a canoe and plucks him out of the water. In her arms, he becomes a baby. Her hair is thick and black. It wraps around her body, an endless sari that flows out and over the boat, as if her hair is the ocean. He looks up at her and gurgles. "*Babu*," she says, stroking his cheek. "I am here." She ties the baby to her body, using her hair as a sling. She reaches down for the paddles then speeds them away toward the Eastern horizon, and Mansoor falls into a peaceful sleep. *Shanti, shanti, shanti.*

Chapter 23

CLOSE TO BANFF NATIONAL PARK, Ashif pulls into a gas station. He hadn't expected to drive out this far.

A gas station attendant steps up to his car.

"Fill?" he asks when Ashif slides open the window, his breath visible in the frosty air.

"Yes, thanks," he says, lifting a lever to pop open the gas tank.

The attendant pulls out a small bottle of water branded with a smiling tiger on it. "On the house."

Ashif takes the bottle then reaches for the envelope with Shafina's letter tucked between the windshield and dashboard.

"And don't forget this is in here," Al-Karim said, waving the car registration and insurance in the air before tucking it back in the glove compartment. Ashif nodded. Al-Karim dangled the keys off a finger. Ashif reached for them, but Al-Karim jerked them away at the last second. "You're sure you can drive, right?"

"Of course." Ashif rolled his eyes. "I'm sixteen." He got his licence out and held it up to Al-Karim. The photograph showed Ashif wearing a beret, a shadow of a moustache on his upper lip, his smile wide and silver with braces. He had taken the driver's test the week after his birthday and passed. When Al-Karim heard the news, he made a pact with Ashif. He would lend him his car for an evening in exchange for a promise: Shafina wouldn't tell her father where Arzeen was—his basement apartment.

Ashif and Shafina discussed options for their night out. A Beauty Salon field trip. Maybe a movie—they both wanted to see *The Fly*. Or else, a fancy dinner at 4th Street Rose or maybe Tokyo Sushi—neither one of them had tried sushi before. Or they could explore the art galleries along Seventeenth Avenue. In the end, Shafina decided it would be too risky for her to venture out in public. Someone might report her to her father. "Let's just go to Fish Creek Park and hang out," she said with a glint in her eye, and it was exactly what he wanted, too.

He parked the car in an empty lot close to the creek. It was dark except for the soft glow of street lamps.

"Look what I got today!" she said, handing him a university course calendar. "McGill." She was in an ivory ruffled blouse that billowed out over her painter jeans and a red plaid tie that hung loose around the collar.

"Cool!"

They had decided to keep their plans a secret. For now. Their families didn't have the money to send them away, and if they heard the subjects they wanted to study or the careers they were considering, they would have never approved. His mother would never have said anything. She was proud of his education no matter how well or how poorly he did. It was his father who would be the problem. "Who goes to university to get a job that pays nothing? What kind of investment is that? Utter waste of time and money, son." Ashif understood. He didn't want to live below the poverty line, either. But he also didn't need to make a lot of money. He had another aim: a life centred on beauty and meaning. Moderation, too. But how could he explain an idea like that to a man like his father? So, he decided to bide his time, tell his father only when he and Shafina were ready to make their getaway.

They could take out student loans, but they were both strong students and hoped to win scholarships to fund their way. For the Aga Khan Foundation, they decided to play it safe. They'd mark down business as their major. Although the foundation was open to any major, they weren't sure who was on the scholarship committee. What if someone on it knew one of their parents? They didn't want to risk word leaking out.

Shafina slipped off her glasses and leaned in to him. Her tongue was warm and wet. He pulled her closer and let his mouth sink into hers. She wiggled a hand up between their bodies, unbuttoned her blouse for him. Her breasts were small and shapely, her nipples pale pink. As he moved to touch her, he saw his mother's breasts, the dark coins of her nipples as she buttoned her nightgown on her way out of his father's room. He yanked Shafina's hands down from his neck.

"Hey, what's wrong?" she asked.

He slumped into the car seat and turned to the window to see the dense and dark forest of trees. "I don't think we should . . ."

Shafina tugged playfully at his T-shirt. "Don't feel shy, *mon chéri*." She took his hands and guided them to her breasts. "It's my first time, too."

"He needs us, *bheta*," his mother had said to Ashif, pulling her hair forward to cover her healing bruises. He looked at Shafina, now, half-naked in front of him, and felt the same hot ember of rage ignite inside him. How many times has she done this before? Whore! He felt a sudden urge to spit at her. He pushed her away and rushed out of the car, slamming the door shut.

He stood gripping the lamppost, beating his head lightly but insistently against the metal. All he could see was his mother in her nightgown, her face swollen and bruised, her pendulous, submissive breasts.

"What's wrong, *mon chéri*?" Shafina asked, coming up from behind him to touch the small of his back.

A hot lava cut through him. He whipped around and grabbed her by the arms. He shook her violently and flung her aside.

Then, he heard the clanging of garbage cans, and Shafina was on the ground, in a sea of garbage. Only then did his rage subside. Only then did he understand what he had done.

He was overcome with shame. Until then, he felt as if he'd been hovering above himself, watching a horror movie. Not in it. He rushed to her side. "I'm sorry, *ma chérie*. I don't know what—"

Shafina threw his hands off her. "Get away from me!"

He could see in her eyes that she thought he was a monster. He turned and walked back to the lamppost. Under the hard cone of light, he examined his hands, turned them from side to side. The hands that hurt Shafina. Hands that were broad and powerful like his father's hands. Hands that tossed him up into the air, swung him over pools of melted snow, stroked his hair as he lay in the crook of his arm, a newspaper spread between the great expanse of those hands; hands laid over his as he learned to steer a car. Hands that became fists. His mother beaten to the ground. Shafina on the ground.

Hateful hands. He punched at the lamppost lightly, then again and again, a growing frenzy of fists, as if fighting someone. He wanted to bring him down. Punish him. Make him pay.

"Ashif! Don't!" Shafina shrieked, scrambling up from the ground.

He couldn't stop. He punched and he punched. "I hate you," he said over and over again. Blood dripped down the lamppost.

"Please stop! You're hurting yourself!"

The more it hurt, the better he felt. He deserved it.

"Please, Ashif." Shafina reached for his shoulder. "Look at me."

He stopped, but he wouldn't turn around. He kept his head down and started to walk away, slowly at first, then faster and faster.

"Don't leave me alone here," Shafina cried. "I can't drive!"

Ashif couldn't stop. He ran through the parking lot and into the park. He ran along the winding trails, his hands broken and bleeding. "Coward!" a voice in the trees called after him. "You just stood there and watched. You did nothing to stop him."

"What kind of man are you? A sissy boy, that's what!"

"No, I'm not!" Ashif yelled.

"Yes, you are!"

"I wanted to stop him," he whimpers. But he couldn't move. As if he'd been injected with anesthetic. His body was frozen in place.

Faster and faster he ran, through more trails and trees. But the voice would not stop. It gained speed. Chased him down and toppled him. Climbed on top, crushed his chest. He tried to fight, but it was too strong. He gasped for air. Above him, the stars began to fade. His voice, too. "Please, don't . . ." It only pressed harder. Until all the air was out of him. Until there was nothing. Only silence.

Ashif slips a finger under the flap of the envelope Arzeen gave him and opens the email from Shafina.

From: Shafina Dawood [mailto: s.dawood@aljazeera.com]
Sent: Thursday, January 22, 1998
To: Arzeen Walji
Subject: For Ashif

Dear Ashif,

I'm really sorry that we are reconnecting over such sad
news. Arzeen told me about the passing of your father.
I'm so sorry for your loss. Please give your mother my
deepest condolences. I'm sad I never had a chance to
meet your father. But I remember how fondly you spoke
of him. How much you missed him. He was living in
Rocky Mountain House the years we were together.

I have such good memories of our time together. I hope
you do, too. Remember the list of must-visit cities we made
on our study room wall after reading *Around the World
in Eighty Days*? New York, Buenos Aires, Mexico City,
Isfahan, Luxor, Cape Town, Aleppo, Paris, and on and on!
(Five down, a zillion to go!) I still have the library copy
of *The Conference of the Birds*. Imagine the fine on that!
And here's what's crazy: the B.S. cover is still intact and
so is our insert of the Faiz poem. I wonder if our sweet
old librarian-in-arms, Mrs. Sims, is still there? She'd be
105 by now! All of that seems like so long ago. Yet so recent.
I wonder how you are. Where you are. What you're doing.

You've crossed my mind so many times over the
years—and sometimes at the most random moments.

Like the other day on the subway. Through the gaps of bodies on the packed train, I spotted this guy. He had his back turned to me. All I could see was his head, his neck. Then I noticed he had the same stubborn cowlick as you. The same Q shape. The same darkness. The same thickness. It made me smile. It reminded me that wherever you were in the world, we were still under the same sky.

I wasn't sure if I should write to you but I decided I needed to. I don't know what happened for you that night, in the park. That night broke everything I knew about you, about us. About me, too. At first, I wondered if it had really happened or not. I was hurt and confused by it. Angry, too.

I was sure we would talk about it—work through it together. We could always speak about anything. Everything. But you shut me out—and that added to my pain and anger. You wouldn't even take my phone calls. Then I heard you moved to Toronto for business school. None of it made sense and when my heart softened, I came to a new thought. There must have been something going on for you at home that I didn't know about. My heart broke for you even if I knew what you did was wrong.

Soon after, I was on my way to the Sorbonne. In Paris, I thought I could forget about that night, but I haven't been able to shake it. It's followed me all these years. Haunted me, even. Affected some of my relationships. I had a hard time trusting men after.

I'm hoping you might be open to speaking to me about that night and the things that followed? I want to make sense of it and let it go. Maybe you want that, too?

You can write to me at this email. Or if you're planning to be in NYC, let me know. I'm going to be here for a few more months covering the Abdul Rehman case. I'd be happy to meet you here.

I'll sign off with a poem. Rumi, of course. ☺

Out beyond ideas of wrongdoing and rightdoing,
there is a field. I'll meet you there.

I hope we can find a way there,
Shafina

Shafina Dawood, Photojournalist
Aljazeera News (Cairo Bureau)
9 Mathaf El Manial St.
Cairo, Egypt

The gas station attendant raps on the window.

"How you paying, mister?" he asks when Ashif rolls down the window.

Ashif can't answer. Something inside him cracks like ice across a frozen lake, and, for the first time since his father's death, he begins to cry uncontrollably. He stuffs a few bills into the attendant's hand and shifts into drive.

"Hang on," the attendant calls after him. "Your change . . ."

By the time Ashif pulls the car over to the side of the highway, his legs are shaking. His face is wet with tears. His neck, too. He steps out onto the embankment. Below him there is a valley wrapped by snow-peaked mountains. An emerald-green lake at the bottom. He falls to his knees in anguish. He stays like this for a while, kneeling at the valley like an altar. When he finally stands up, his knees are patches of wet snow.

Ashif scurried alongside his father, trying to keep up. He was barely five. Both of them on their knees, as they rolled the massive ball of snow. Round and round, down a field in the park. Like a boulder. They only stopped when it was big enough for the base of the snowman's body. Their first one. They rolled a smaller one for his middle, then another for his head. His father also brought along a paper bag with a carrot for the nose, bottle caps for the eyes and mouth.

"He's so handsome," a woman said when they were done. She and her daughter were building their own snowman a few feet away.

"He's our first snowman!" Ashif declared.

"That's special," she said then turned to her daughter. "Isn't that special, honey?"

"Uh-huh," the girl said.

"Why don't I take a picture?" the woman asked, pulling out a Polaroid camera from her knapsack.

"Sure!" Ashif said.

"That's very nice of you," Mansoor added.

The woman was about to snap the picture when Mansoor stopped her. "One second." He pulled out a small flag from a paper bag. "Come, son. You do it," he said.

"Smile!" the woman said.

Moments later, the camera spit out the picture. She waved it dry then handed it to Ashif. Like magic, an image of him and his father surfaced inside the frame. Ashif in his father's arms, the two of them gazing at each other and laughing. Both of them in snowsuits and mukluks, like spacesuits. Their arms up in victory. A Canadian flag planted in the snowman's head as big as the moon.

He dusts the snow from his pants and gazes one last time at the mountains, the valley, the lake below. "Please take care of my father," he tells the mountains. He instinctively touches the tip of his index finger to his nose then his chin, a gesture made at the end of a prayer.

He returns to his car and pulls onto the highway. He's not sure where the route goes, but it winds up the mountain toward the sky.

He doesn't realize how far he has driven until he sees the sign reading WELCOME TO THE COLUMBIA ICEFIELD. The face of the mountain is covered with wire mesh. A yellow sign flashes CAUTION: ROCK SLIDES.

He pulls into a gravel parking lot at the base of the mountain. It's empty except for a few cars. It looks vaguely familiar, then he remembers. A grade two field trip. Ms. Clarke. He hasn't been here since.

He steps out of his car, shields his eyes from the afternoon sun, and surveys the mountain. The glacier seemed so much bigger, so much grander when he saw it as a child. He turns back to the highway and double-checks the sign. It's the right place. Strange. He remembers the ice sheet sweeping down from the top of the mountain to the edge of the parking lot in one uninterrupted mass. Now, the ice sheet stops halfway up the mountain, like a blanket that's been yanked up from the other side. Below the ice, there's only a jumble of exposed rock and rubble like a quarry. He reaches in for the bottle of water, tucks it into his jacket, and follows the arrows to the trailhead.

A giant handrail with dates and a sign, THIS IS WHERE THE GLACIER WAS, runs along the trail. It starts at 1970. He hikes up the rocky path to 1980, the year he would have been here, and continues until he arrives at 1998, eighteen years later. Here, the icecap is cordoned off by a yellow plastic banner, like police tape. A couple of tourists stand at the border between ice and rock, snapping photographs. Another sits on the jagged edge of the ice sheet bundled in a parka, her feet dangling under her.

Ashif glances back down the trail. He's in awe. A massive body retreating slowly but steadily. A centimetre, maybe a millimetre, every day until one day it's gone, quietly disappearing into water. He feels a strange sense of sadness and loss. He lowers himself onto a boulder and focuses his gaze upward, past the yellow tape, to where he can see only snow and ice. A mass of white.

A bus with tracks for tires, like a Zamboni, ferried Ashif's class up the mountain. It crawled over the ice like a giant caterpillar. Ms. Clarke stood at the front bundled in a knee-length downfilled jacket, red curls sticking out from under her green wool toque.

"Okay, people. Listen up," she said, swaying to and fro even as she held on to the railing above her. She always called them people, not kids or children like the other teachers. Ashif liked that. Ashif liked her. She was his favourite teacher ever.

Ms. Clarke explained that a glacier was actually a long, deep river of ice and the melting ice flowed down through a system of other rivers, right into three oceans.

Near the top of the mountain, the driver stopped and pulled open the giant doors. Ms. Clarke led the children out. Ashif, dressed in his snowsuit and mukluks, jumped out of the bus and landed firmly on the ice like an astronaut on the moon.

"Over here, people," Ms. Clarke called, hugging a stack of notebooks to her chest.

Ashif stood apart from the cluster of kids and gazed up at the mountain. He felt tiny, as if he wasn't even an inch tall.

"Okay! Here's your assignment." Ms. Clarke passed out a notebook to everyone. "I want you to imagine that you are scientists here to understand and explore this glacier. Your job is to record what you see and report back." She then waved them away. "Okay, off you go. But stay where I can see you, people."

The children scattered across the ice, some in pairs, others in groups, a few, like Ashif, on their own. Small, colourful dots scurrying across a giant field of white.

Ashif trekked across the ice sheet, slowly and carefully, not because he was afraid. He was in awe. All he could see was snow and ice, the entire earth was pure white. He twirled around for a full view, then again. And again. Slowly at first, then faster and faster, his arms stretched out, round and round, until he fell to his knees, laughing and dizzy.

He lay down on the glacier. Pressed his ear to it. He listened, like a doctor, for a heartbeat. He heard the sound of water gushing below him. An ocean! He lifted himself off the ice. Absolute silence and stillness. He dropped his head down again—gushing water. He couldn't believe it. Underneath the silence of the ice, there was another world. He was overcome by the thought. He scanned the surface of the ice for a crack and when he found one, he crawled over on his belly.

He cupped his hands around his face and peered in. In the thin blue light, he could see caves of ice carved into beautiful and strange shapes. Light bounced off their glassy walls and refracted into thousands of rainbows. Below him, a green pool like a mirror. He threw off a mitten and stretched his arm down, grazed his fingers over his watery self. This made him laugh so much, he cried.

"Time to go, Ashif."

He gazed up from the ice to see Ms. Clarke with a halo of sunshine around her.

He stood up reluctantly. "But we only just got here."

"We've been here for over an hour."

"Really?" It had felt like minutes.

"What were you doing?" Ms. Clarke asked.

"Listening to the ice!" he told her excitedly.

"That's so lovely. What did it tell you?"

"So many things." He went on to tell her about the magical world underneath.

"That's beautiful, Ashif. No one's reported that before," she said, her smile as warm as the sun. "Make sure you put it in your journal, okay?"

"Okay. I'm like Neil Armstrong, right? I go where no man has gone before," he said with hands on his hips like his father.

"Yes, you are." She laughed. "But instead of outer space, you can be a great explorer of inner space."

"Yes!" He jumped up and down. "That's what I'm going to be."

Ashif walks to the edge of the ice to where he and Ms. Clarke once were. He leans down and peers under the ice. Water gushes under the surface. He gets the bottle of water from his jacket pocket, empties it out, and then reaches his hand under the stream and fills the bottle.

By the time he wanders back to the parking lot, the afternoon sun is low in the horizon, casting a pinkish glow over the mountains. He unlocks the back door of the car, slips off his coat, and throws it in. The seat and floor are covered with his father's odometer log books, the ones he had hoped were diaries. Is this the only record of his father's life? Then he thinks of his own life. What if there was an odometer recording his journeys? The endless kilometres of running, from everything and everyone. Running and running, but he never gets anywhere. Like running on the spot. He can't get away. Not even from himself.

He sits heavily in the driver's seat. He uncaps the bottle of glacial water and tips it back, empties it. He's never felt this parched in his life. He shifts the car into drive and begins his journey home.

Chapter 24

LAYLA CONSIDERS WAKING ASHIF. It's still early, but he was fast asleep when she came home from jamatkhana with Shamma and Almas at nine last night. She decides to let him rest. He must need it. She has been up for hours. She couldn't sleep, but she also wanted to start cooking for the *bhati*, the wake that would normally take place right after the funeral. The Mayat and Ghusal Committee always takes care of feeding the *jamat*, but she wanted to contribute a dish and they accepted.

She pours holy water from a perfume-shaped bottle into an Arabic teacup. She cradles the *pyali* in her palms, one over the other, shuts her eyes and asks Allah to please forgive her sins. She then throws her head back and swallows the *niyaz* in one gulp, as if it's medicine, and it is. Holy water heals the body.

Arzeen asked Layla if she wanted to be present when they pulled Mansoor's life support. Layla was distraught by the idea, but said yes. She wanted to be with her husband when he passed from this world to the next. Mukhi Sahib came with her. He arrived earlier to give her his support and also perform the *chanta*-holy water ceremony on Mansoor's body. But first, he suggested she take a few minutes alone with him.

Layla started crying the moment she saw her husband. He was hooked up to a tube that pumped air into his throat. His chest moved up and down as if he was breathing. His skin was yellow and blistered. His face, swollen. His hands and feet, his toes and fingers, too. But what startled her were his bruises. A patchwork of blue and black all over his body as though he had been in a boxing ring last night, not a farm field. She grasped the railing on his bed. Suddenly, she began to tremble. In her mind's eye, his bruises became her bruises, her broken face.

She couldn't believe he had done that to her. She slept in Ashif's room that night and for many nights· after, trying to forget the truth. But her body wouldn't let her. The pain of a reopened cut on her lip, a bruise on her cheek, her swollen eye, reminded her daily. How could he have done this to her? Was it her fault? Mansoor never said it was, but she could feel it. He blamed her. So did everyone else who saw her. The stares and whispers. She must have done something to deserve that! She started believing it, too. A deep shame washed over her. She stayed home, hid herself from view.

Shamma and Almas said she should leave him. But where would she go? She did not have the money and, more than that, she refused to break her family apart. Instead, she hoped he would never do it again. Told herself he wouldn't. But she constantly worried he might and a new fear settled into her stomach, like layers of sediment at the bottom of a lake. She was now more careful about what she said, more careful about what she did. She made herself smaller and smaller. Quieter and quieter. She didn't trust him. She didn't trust herself, either. What if she made the same mistake again?

She looked at her husband's limp body. "No!" she suddenly blurted out. He couldn't hurt her. Not anymore. He was powerless. "It wasn't my fault. It was yours!" She shook with anger. "You had no right to do what you did to me. I didn't do anything wrong. I was only telling you my opinion. I have the right to do that. I am your wife. The mother of your son. You broke my body that night, but you remained broken for years." Hot tears dripped down her face. "What you did to me was wrong. Very wrong. And nothing justifies it. Nothing."

Arzeen inched open the door. "May we come in, Aunty?"

Layla took a few moments to compose herself. "Yes." She was exhausted. But she felt lighter, too. As though the sludgy fear had somehow been drained from her body.

Arzeen walked in. Mukhi Sahib, as well. In his hands, he held a bowl of holy water.

"You understand you are the surrogate repentant, Layla *Bai*?" he asked and Layla nodded. "Please, come forward a little, Layla *Bai*," Mukhi said. He stood on the opposite side of the bed.

Layla pressed her palms together and leaned over Mansoor's body. "Dear Imam, on behalf of my husband, I beg you to please forgive his sins, known and unknown." Her legs trembled against the bed, her voice shook.

Mukhi dipped his fingers into the bowl. "He is forgiven," he said, spraying Layla's face with the holy water. Then, he sprayed Mansoor's face. He repeated the ablution: Layla's face, Mansoor's face. Layla. Mansoor.

"Dear Imam, on behalf of my husband, I beg you to please forgive all his sins, known and unknown." Layla's eyes filled with tears.

Mukhi dipped his fingers into the water. "He is forgiven." Layla's face, Mansoor's face's. Layla. Mansoor. Layla, Mansoor.

"Dear Imam, on behalf of my husband, I beg you to please forgive his sins, known and unknown."

"He is forgiven. He is forgiven. He is forgiven." Layla. Mansoor. Layla, Mansoor. LaylaMansoor.

Mukhi reached over the bed and held a crystal rock of sugar at her mouth. She wiped her palms over her wet face, and let the sweetness fill her mouth.

"Should I start, Aunty?" Arzeen asked.

Layla nodded.

Arzeen pushed some buttons, turned some knobs, and unhooked the tubes. The machines beeped and flashed. Mansoor's body convulsed. His eyes popped open, locked onto Layla's. Layla lifted his hand to her mouth and kissed it. "Rest in peace, my husband. You are forgiven." Mansoor took his final breath, then closed his eyes.

Layla dusts the kitchen counter with a little more flour. She spreads a square of dough on top and gently presses her rolling pin over it. Slow-slow-quick-quick-slow. Until the *pur* is paper-thin. Then she scoops a spoonful of spiced minced chicken from a massive steel bowl and massages it into the middle of the square. She dips a finger into a jar of melted ghee, lifts one corner of the delicate pastry, and folds it, like a flap of an envelope, over the mound of meat. She continues like this, gently pulling and tugging at each corner, until she is satisfied with the shape. She flips the perfect triangle over in her palms and pats it with a little more ghee, before setting it on the growing pyramid of samosas. She wants enough to feed everyone at the wake.

She is also cooking Mansoor's favourite dishes—a tradition many don't follow anymore. She will take the platters to jamatkhana tonight, where they will be auctioned off at *naandi*, the nightly offering of food. She knows her husband's tastes well, as if they are her own. A pinch more salt in the dhar lentils, a little less chili in the masala fish, one-quarter finger of cumin in the cauliflower curry, medium-thick consistency for the beef curry, a handful and a bit of coriander for the meat pies, two-and-a-half fingers of mashed potatoes for the Indian shepherd's pie. Recipes she has tailored over thirty years of marriage, memorized by heart. She thinks of all the meals she and Mansoor have had together. Hundreds. Thousands. More. Her heart aches. She asks the Imam to please deliver this food to Mansoor, to help make this, his final journey, as easy and comfortable as possible. Amen.

A pot of semolina, Carnation milk, and cardamom bubbles on the stove. A soft, sweet dessert. Ashif loved it as a child. So did she. So would have Maryam. Her sweet little Maryam. She scoops out a few spoonfuls of *siro* into a glass finger bowl and presses it into a mound. She decorates it with a heart of raisins then wraps it in plastic and sets it down next to the growing cluster of Mansoor's dishes. She asks her husband to find their girl. You will recognize her, she tells him. She has a red birthmark shaped like a star on her shoulder. She'd seen it those few minutes she'd been allowed to hold her. Please give her a tasting. Tell her it's from her mother. Tell her she is dearly missed. That she is in my heart and prayers daily. Ismaili or not. She is a child of God and that is enough. More than enough.

Chapter 25

WHEN ASHIF WAKES UP over ten hours later, he's famished. It's still dark outside. It takes him a few minutes to remember where he is. Calgary. His bedroom. Then he remembers. His father. The funeral.

He gets out of bed and steps on a pile of clothes, like shed skin, on the floor. He reaches for his pants, slips them on, but decides against the shirt and suit jacket. The letter from Shafina falls out from his pants pocket. He doesn't want to lose her contact information. He gets his cellphone out and punches in her email address. Her phone number, too. He doesn't know what he'll say—or how to speak about it. But he knows this much. He wants to tell her how deeply sorry he is for hurting her. For running away that night. For never reaching out to her after. For pretending it never happened. Forgetting it did. He's been lying to himself all these years. He wants to face the truth. For her. For himself.

He roots through the room's closet where he finds a Duran Duran T-shirt. He tries it on. It looks silly—it's so small. He laughs at himself, tosses it back. He grabs a larger white T-shirt instead.

He finds Layla at the stove in the kitchen. "Did you sleep okay, Mummy?"

"Oh, good, you are up, *bheta*," she says, setting a wooden spoon down.

"You let me sleep for so long."

"I didn't want to disturb you. You were sleeping so nicely." She turns down the stove's element and wipes her hands down the front of her apron.

They embrace tightly.

She pushes him back to look at him. "You must be hungry, no?"

"So hungry."

"Sit-sit. Let me give you food."

"What about you? Have you eaten?" Ashif asks.

She shakes her head, pulling a Tupperware container out of the fridge.

He takes the container from her. "Let's eat together. Before the sun rises, for your fast."

"Yes, okay." She hugs him again.

She reaches into the fridge for another container and another, passing each one to Ashif, as if on an assembly line. He sets each on the kitchen table and soon the surface is covered with containers. He clumsily snaps off the lids; some fly off the table.

"Slowly, *bheta*," she says, smiling.

"I'm so hungry!" He feels as if he hasn't eaten in days.

They start with the *paya*. Layla scoops the goats-feet curry into a serving bowl and warms it in the microwave. When it's ready, they sit down. They devour the meat, sucking out the marrow. Orange sauce drips down Ashif's chin. When they finish the *paya*, they dig into the vegetable *pilau*, then the *ondwoh*, scooping out the savoury cake with their fingers, then the cardamom-nut rice pudding. They continue like this, moving from dish to dish, eating and eating, until they finally sit back in their chairs, their wrists resting on the edge of their plates.

"It's all so good," he says, really meaning it, as if he's tasting his mother's food for the first time.

He's never said the words before, but now they come out unexpectedly. "I love you."

"I love you, too," she says then lets out a burp.

They both laugh. Then, they sit in silence.

"Are you still hungry?" he finally asks.

"Yes!"

"Me, too," he says and reaches for the serving spoon.

They empty the pot of *siro*, devouring every grain of sweetness.

When they clean up, Ashif notices the samosas. "You made chicken samosas?" he asks incredulously.

"Yes, why not? Let everyone enjoy," she says, certain that the Imam, in his great benevolence, will stay by her side. Ashif's, too. With or without a vow. His love for his spiritual children was unconditional. Like her love for her children.

There's a knock at the front door. Shamma and Almas. They've come to help her fry the samosas, then take them to the wake for her. They had recently purchased an old pink Cadillac, which they had painted with the words THE PINK

COMB, A SHIVJI SISTERS ENTERPRISE. A business writeoff, Almas explained, though they planned to use it mostly for weekend excursions and summer holidays. The back was already rigged, like a motor home, with a gas hook-up and a hotel-sized fridge. Layla was invited, they told her, to join them anytime she wanted.

"Go lie down on your bed, Layla," Shamma insists. "We will finish it."

Almas and Ashif agree. They know she didn't sleep much last night and she'd stayed up the night before on Lailatul Qadr. She refuses to go to her bedroom, but agrees to rest on the couch. "This way I can supervise you two," she says, and everyone laughs.

Ashif wanders into the living room where his mother is asleep on the couch. He picks up the wool blanket that's on the floor and covers her. He walks to his father's desk in the far corner of the living room. It's perfectly organized. The pens, the files, the magazines. In the middle of the desk—two copies of his father's business plan. One is labelled AMV. The other, MGV. He picks up his copy and sets it on a reading chair.

He slips on his winter coat and steps outside. The tiny back-yard is a mound of snow. The air is crisp but the prairie sky is a boundless blue. A small bird flies down from the sky and lands on a leafless tree. Her body is brilliant blue; her crown golden. The branch vibrates like the string of an instrument and she begins to sing. Ashif takes a deep breath. Lets out a cough. It's rough and dry, like sandpaper on wood. As if his lungs aren't used to air, as if this is his first breath. Inhale. Exhale. Inhale.

Works Cited

"Don't pretend to be a candle, be a moth."

Jalaludin Rumi, "Whispers of Love" (translated by Kabir Helminski), from *The Rumi Collection*. Boston, MA: Shambhala Publications, Inc., 1998. Page 136.

"You are an ocean in a drop of dew."

Jalaludin Rumi (translated by Coleman Barts), from *Rumi: The Book of Love: Poems of Ecstasy and Longing*. New York, NY: HarperOne, 2003. Page 63.

"Out beyond ideas of wrongdoing and rightdoing,/there is a field. I'll meet you there."

Jalaludin Rumi, "Soul, Heart, and Body One Morning" (translated by Coleman Barks), from *Rumi: The Book of Love: Poems of Ecstasy and Longing*. New York, NY: HarperOne, 2003. Page 123.

"Strong spirits transcend rules."

Prince in "Genius in short." by Barney Hoskyns, from *The Guardian*. Web. 19 Feb 2006.

Acknowledgments

THIS BOOK TRAVELLED OVER several countries and many years to get here. My deepest, heartfelt gratitude to all those who were on this journey with me.

Rajinderpal S. Pal, whose presence in my life makes everything better. This book, too. Ann Shin, who was with me even when there were thousands of miles between us. Gerardo Ruiz, por arbrir tu mundo y mi corazón, y darle a este libro un lugar de refugio.

Marguerite Pigeon and Karim Ladak, without whom I could have never started this book. Lawrence Hill, who mentored me early on. Merilyn Simonds, who guided me through that elusive first draft. David Chariandy, for his kindness and support, and for cheering me on to the finish line.

At Penguin Random House, Nicole Winstanley, Deborah Sun de la Cruz, and Shima Aoki for their editorial acuity. My agent, Hilary McMahon, for her patience.

A special thank you to my family, especially my parents, Nurali and Rozina Mohamedali, for their constant love and support; my niece and co-conspirator, Salina Rasul, for her uncommon empathy and understanding. My friends, near and far, for sustaining me, especially Jessica Adams, Derek Burrows, Isaura Contreras, Kathy Kissik, Rashmi & Vanita Varma, and Jonathan Watton. Also, Jim Fleck, for his support and genuine understanding of a writer's life.

The Canada Council for the Arts, the Ontario Arts Council, and the Toronto Arts Council for their generous support. The Banff Centre for the Arts, the Millay Colony for the Arts in New York, and Fundación Valparaíso in Spain for the time and space to write.

This book is a work of fiction and if there are inaccuracies with any details or historical facts, they are my own.